Y020020

Glyn E .... *brae*, is
publish......................................y Editor
of Issue 11 of *The Lonely Crowd* and was included in the Verve
Press anthology, *84*.

Rose Widlake was the inaugural winner of the Terry
Hetherington Young Writers Award in 2009, and became a
trustee of the award in 2015. She has worked for Parthian
Books and Candy Jar Books, and currently works for the
Royal College of Music as its Trust and Foundations Manager.
Originally from Neath, she now lives in London.

Molly Holborn is the co-author of a children's book,
Moonbeam's Arctic Adventure, published by Y Lolfa. She is
currently studying English Literature and Creative Writing at
Swansea University, whilst working at Parthian Books. She is
originally from Cwmbran.

D1643353

Also available

Cheval 12

Edited by Glyn Edwards,
Molly Holborn and Rose Widlake

Foreword by Aida Birch

Parthian, Cardigan SA43 1ED
www.parthianbooks.com
ISBN 978-1-912681-43-3
First published in 2019 © the contributors
Edited by Glyn Edwards, Molly Holborn and Rose Widlake
Cover design by www.theundercard.co.uk
Cover image: Rose Horridge www.rosehorridgeart.co.uk
Typeset by Elaine Sharples www.typesetter.org.uk
Printed by 4edge Limited

Contents

Foreword

by Aida Birch

It is very rewarding for the Trustees of the Terry Hetherington Young Writers Award to continue with the ambition of the late Terry Hetherington by promoting new, young writers. Many previous prize winners have had their own collection of poetry and short stories published. Past prize winners, their submissions and book titles can be found on the cheval website: www.chevalwriters.org.uk.

Malcolm Lloyd provides an all-encompassing website that highlights the talents of young writers who continue to form a social network. The Terry Hetherington Facebook pages reveal postings from all parts of Wales and abroad.

Ongoing funding depends on the monthly support from contributors who attend Cheval Neath Poems and Pints at the Cambrian Arms in Neath. Recordings of the young writers who read at the awards evenings and the performances of Poems and Pints contributors can also be found on the website.

The First Prize-winner was Eleanor Howe for her poem 'The Fox' where she writes: 'A fine country fox you are/full fattish scarlet'. The poet has a rare eye for every movement, and one judge commented: 'The characterisation of the fox is wonderful.'

The Second Prize-winner for fiction was 'The Humiliation of Basboosa' by Cynan Llwyd. It is an absorbing story: the writer has style and a deep understanding of other cultures.

One judge commented: 'I particularly liked the switch of perspective at the end.'

The Second Prize-winner for poetry was Nathan Munday, for his poem: 'At Last'. It was described by one judge as 'A poem with good perspective of freedom and reality.' Nathan beautifully described the poem's setting, writing 'The man-made archipelago expands like plastic'.

The Highly Commended poet, Morgan Owen, takes the reader from an industrial sense of place to a prior rural area in his poem 'Dowlais Dream', where he writes 'It is here, to this salient of green / needling along the road.'

Cheval 12 contains moving poetry and compelling fiction with an abundance of literary skill.

Two previous prize winners demonstrate how they continue to reflect on their own creative talents. Katya Johnson has a lively story and takes the reader to 'Folly Farm', whilst Eluned Gramich presents a fascinating and compelling story, 'After the Stag'.

Two of the 2018 prize winners, Katya Johnson and Thomas Tyrrell, were able to benefit from attending an 'Emerging Writers Course' at Ty Newydd Writing Centre in Gwynedd. Bursaries were awarded from Literature Wales and Parthian Books. Through group workshops they benefitted from enhancing their knowledge of editing and publishing. This was an added bonus for the prize-winners.

'Linkage', the poem included in *Cheval 12*, by Terry Hetherington, was created following a visit when his grandson named Troy was three years of age. It was a beautiful moon-lit evening during the summer-time. He held Troy's hand and pointed to the moon, directing his 'gaze to the heavens'. Terry realised that to Troy, the moon was part of his world – a cosmic link – writing, 'Your body folds down / as you touch some life I do not see.'

It is rewarding to receive so many entries for the 2019 Terry Hetherington Young Writers Award. For the young writers who are not included in *Cheval 12*, it is as disappointing for the judges as it is for the contributors. All the entries have been of a high standard and we encourage all the young writers to send an entry for the 2020 award.

Preface

by Rose Widlake

This was a strong year for entries and it was a joy to edit this book with Molly and Glyn. It was a delight to delve into the judge's pack and open up a pandora's box of voices from emerging writers.

There were a lot of recurring themes and subjects — broken hearts, miners, life in the valleys, witches, the end of the world and foxes. Some of the works based on these themes and subjects have made it into *Cheval* (and notably, Eleanor Howe has won First Prize with her excellent poem 'The Fox'). The uncertain times we live in have seeped into stories and poems which experiment with form and grapple with different time periods, characters and universes. One thing that is certain is that there is a lot of talent emerging from young writers who live in and come from Wales.

For some of the writers, this is their first time in print. It is exciting to see what they will write next, what their voice will grow to become. Many of the writers have been published in *Cheval* before, and their voices grow stronger each year. It is a testament to the award (and the wonderful Aida Birch) that so many writers return.

The award itself has come such a long way, too. From the first *Cheval* books (lovingly printed out on to sheets of A4 in black and white and stapled in the middle) to now, a paperback published by Parthian.

So many people are involved in the *Cheval* family, and the brood is growing every year. There are the people who drop a few pounds in the tin when they go to Poems and Pints (and those who do so every month), the people with previous editions of *Cheval* tucked on their bookshelves, the writers, the trustees, Malcolm the website wiz, Parthian, the team at the Dylan Thomas Centre. At the centre of it all is Terry, a man from Neath who wrote poems and encouraged other people in the town to do the same, and Aida, who stays up well past midnight sending personalised emails to every person who enters their work into the award. *Cheval* is so much more than the sum of its parts but when you break it down each part is bloody beautiful.

We hope you enjoy this year's edition of *Cheval*. If you're new here, welcome to the family.

Terry Hetherington

Linkage (For Troy)

In the peculiar pull of the bloodline,
I have shared a measure
of your three years existence here,
directing your gaze to the heavens,
and lifting your small frame
to the embrace of foliage.
Rivers you have seen
and the flight of startled birds.
Your body folds down
as you touch some life I do not see.

I know now that all of these are part of you:
you have cleared some dross from my reasoning,
and I am learning to accept with shock
that, perhaps, the metamorphosis
from reality has been mine?
Having, as yet, no concept of retribution,
you wear stars in your hair
and the earth murmurs from your eyes.

Forgive me my looming treachery:
for I too will suck on your purity,
joining my breath
with all who breathe on you;

permeating your senses
with the pungency of our morass.
Until then, permit me your little hand,
warm in mine,
to be my transient cosmic link.

Eleanor Howe

The Fox

1st Prize

a fine country fox you are
full   fattish   scarlet
what evolutionary folly
fired your fur
a   klaxon   in the green

my lumbering gait
sets you off
a   flare
on sheep-gnawed hills too
bare for refuge
you can't resist to turn and look
if I had a gun you'd be

                                  gone

you come back later
to the farmer's field
sloping away from my garden
to tug at the rook-pecked ewe
by the fence
raise my binoculars
to the   flickering   red

you know
look at me square and
run to the scrub
gone again
    I've cost you a meal

I wish I could invite you in
for supper
to apologise
serve you meat at my table
ask you to teach me
the lore of the land
the news from the woods

but surely you would laugh at me —
your teeth and tongue wolfishly
            quivering —
at my soft belly
weak nose
my pots and pans
blankets
and my books

you'd want your meat raw
still bloody-warm with
hard-won life

you would wink past
waggling your brush sassily
all the way to the door

and step into the dark new-mooned lane
bay your eldritch bark

belonging to it

Llynisaf

Dirt tracks —
        dissect the heath, desolate but for
        spongy boulders of bilberry shrubs
        studded with boozy spring flowers
        white starbursts of grass-of-Parnassus
— they are
muscle memories
of a footsore miner, first to rise
beneath pristine pre-dawn moons,
to open the floodgates
at Llyn Isaf
that fed the mine.

From here the height
arrests the valley
basin in stillness.
A dull ribbon, the river,
an inert snakeskin
        ribs of scree
        plunge to meet it
        pleating the hillside with dry streams

that meet in tumuli of grey stones
pockmarking the vale.
Gutted buildings —

rafters exposed
as the angular wing of a
road-killed hawk, erect in the mush —
join the slate-piles

kurgans of men and times past

the valley is as hushed as the grassy leats
that run silently now
from Llyn Isaf.

Nathan Munday

At Last

Runner-Up: Poetry

The orange peel gathers on the desert desk
as post-it notes fuse with strings and stains.
The seconds tick by but the light remains,
as the chariot loses its way
to the west.

The rattling of the A/C machine,
above the shaking trays of tea
moving from the canteen.

The bay-like desks harbour us like boats
anchored on the carpet sea.
We stare at monitors, HD screens –
lighthouses, fooling us
with numbing beams.

The humming A/C machines,
telephones and trolleys,
rattling from the canteen.

This man-made archipelago expands
like a plastic meadow.

Blue tac, stapling, taping – stuck like bic
pens in a crowded pot.
We are free

to worship that A/C Machine.
A deity rumbling above the trolleys.

But there is a time on the flexi sheet which
cuts the chain of this single boat.
He sails the harbour, wears his coat,
and exits with his course set
for the hill.

I cross the road and cattle grid, taking my feet up Cynon's
    edge.
Just me and the breeze, and the wild trees
growing like empires in green colonies.
This exodus home from Pharaoh's lair.
Plucking my harp on a Babylonian stair-
way to Salem.

And then I come to my stile.
It knows my knees.
I bow and worship my Deity.

My office sits still, like a wasp on glass,
My thumb covers its thorny mass,
Now, I can hear bees at last.

Gheorghe and Furnicuţa

My name is Gheorghe. I am a small man from a small country called Moldova where I look after a cow called Furnicuţa. I am unwell with learning, but I am good with animals. I understand the land, the sky, and the Bible.

Every morning, when the dew is frustratingly there – not falling or taken by the ground, just suspended – I grit my teeth and let it touch my ankles a little, as I take Furnicuţa to pasture.

Her breath is cloud and warmth. She is friend and family. When I came from blackness to white, I had no mother. But Furnicuţa has been there. She is quiet like me but hears everything. Her ears move when she walks and her tail flaps when I pat her on the back. She enjoys the little lights in the night, the big day light, and the fresh grass of morning when it stops growing. I am also the same height as her.

I crown her horns with a chain. I prefer it there because I don't like seeing it around her neck. She is Tsarina in her tiara. I don't want to choke her. I go with her in my best cap and outside shoes. She understands me when others find it difficult. I have bad teeth and am not very good with speech. These things are key.

Key. I live with another man called Petru. I live with Petru and two other men in a charity house called *Casa Matei*. We are all unwell with learning. Their names are Petru, Slava, Grişa and Gheorghe. Petru told Gheorghe (that's me) that when he was a baby he swallowed a key, or was it a fish bone? This is the reason for Petru's quietness; only Gheorghe and Dr. Carwyn understand him when he whispers.

The other men live in the house and grow vegetables in the garden. My friend Grişa doesn't grow vegetables because he goes around in a chair with two wheels. He was born in that chair and it has grown with him ever since he was little. Slava wears a blue tie around the house. He is always playing his red pipe which makes him look like a piper.

Gheorghe does not grow vegetables; he looks after Furnicuţa. Once I take Furnicuţa to pasture, I stay awhile with the man who looks after all the village cows, before going home for porridge.

*

Casa Matei is located in a village called Sofia. It has its wells and churches. Baptismal fonts are kitchen bowls, and the gold on the sacred sights dazzles poverty as they queue up to kiss the framed pictures of Andrew and the patriarchs. From the distance, the deep, bass notes of vespers sound like variants of a giant lawnmower. Having kissed the icons, the women peck their children on their cheeks and pat their backsides, before hurrying them along to school.

Sofia was busy that day. The carts, the chickens, and the mothers; even the men had the suggestion of work on their faces. The orthodox priest patrolled the village. He was one of the stranger men of Sofia and was one of the most frightening for Gheorghe. The priest wasn't like Furnicuţa. Yes, they were both black and hairy, but, for Gheorghe, the priest was noisy and moved far too quickly. He would cross himself all the time and shout at animals. He reminded Gheorghe of a pirate. He was a blackened sepulchre and his ship was the big church – an onion-mast galleon full of pictures, booty and no animals; nothing like Noah's ark. Noah was the opposite and had filled his boat with animals. No rainbow crowned that place and there were no animals either, except for the black birds which perched on the crosses of the three towers.

The church sailed on the edge of the village.

Some babushkas would often give Gheorghe the evil eye. In the East, disability is still seen as a curse or an omen. 'His parents were dirty sinners' say some; or 'his grandfather must have been an evil man', according to others. Their scarves mummify their faces. If you remove the layers … yes … deep down … layer by layer – these Matryoshka dolls reveal corpses writhing in the cold. There is no colour then or kindness.

Casa Matei is a haven. Four men live semi-independent lives free from the hellish institutions from which they were rescued. That place was called Badaceni – a bad nightmare. *Casa Matei*, on the other hand, is a place filled with the smell of tomatoes. The swallows are drawn to its rooftops – the garden gives a good view and the heat from inside is nice for birds as well. The founders designed the house by simply injecting the opposite essence of Badaceni into its walls. Cold was swapped with warmth; hunger was replaced with plenty; thirst was dispersed with a clean well; abuse was transformed into blankets; and broken windows were filled with glass, which allowed the men to feel the sun on their faces whilst also remaining warm in winter. Most of all, they were free to sleep and say their prayers without being startled in the darker hours.

Every morning, Gheorghe's job is to leave Furnicuţa with the local cowherd before collecting her from the pasture in the evening. This Moldovan pattern suits him well. The same thing happens again and again.

Many of the houses own a cow but not many owners love their cows like Gheorghe loves Furnicuţa.

*

When Furnicuţa goes to pasture, I sit down and kiss my friend before leaving. She is a hard worker; she is like a bee. She eats so much. That is why she's called Furnicuţa.

She enjoys wild flowers and grasses. This makes good milk like honey – a land flowing with milk and honey.

The soil is her skin. I run my fingers across the ridges. I put my ear to the cold ground and look at the grasses and ants struggling across the leather land. I hear the hum of flies and the yellow black bee landing and flying, landing and flying. I touch the green and follow it until I feel her again.

When we are free, I take the chain from her horns. I am always afraid that another flood will come. God promised that there wouldn't be another one but I don't want Furnicuţa to drift away in case God forgets.

That bad day, it rained very hard so I decided to fetch Furnicuţa earlier than usual.

*

Unbeknown to Gheorghe, the local cowherd had already brought Furnicuţa home because of the downpour. When Gheorghe reached the meadow, the sky's eyelids flickered. In the twilight, he thought he could see her walking away, three meadows in the distance.

The rain stopped as the night folded into a pasture of black. The stars turned into sheep, dotting the dark grasses – wandering and bleating in fields far away. Gheorghe recognised the hunter in the sky who wore his three-studded belt. The sheep were serenading in a moonlight sonata; the music keeping his arrows in the quiver. Gheorghe passed his hand over the sky, transforming the hunter's bow into a shepherd's crook, before joining the stellar dots into a mysterious menagerie. He then combined all the creatures and heroes, closed his eyes, and saw God Himself, arms outstretched, holding the universe together like an ancient professor balancing thirty books between his arms.

When he came to still waters, the sky was reflected in that still, bringing him closer and closer to heaven. His fingers touched the water at the point of starlight leaving heaven lapping at his ankles.

Gheorghe passed the moon. He tipped his cap in recognition of his old friend who had lighted the dark recesses of the institution when he was a child. He was forever in her debt.

He wished that the moon would reveal Furnicuţa to him.

Gheorghe passed the moon again. He smiled sadly at his old acquaintance, hoping that she would shine brighter.

Gheorghe's gentle walk turned into strides.

Strides became a panicked run.

Gheorghe passed the moon and passed it again.

Some farm labourers were smoking under a walnut tree.

13

He waved at them but they stood there like trees, enduring the fresh siege of rain. They weren't interested in this half-wit.

'SSSSo ... Sooo ... Sooo ... ffffff,' Gheorghe stammered.
'Go away! You'll get wet!' The rain was angry and the men were angrier.
'Soooofffffiiiaaa ...' he struggled.
'He's an imbecile. Woof! Woof!'

One of the men barked at Gheorghe like a dog. The others laughed, re-lighting their cigarettes in the rain. Gheorghe ran like a panicked sheep, looking back, running on, looking back, running on ...

He ran to the margin of the village where the three onions sailed on the barking wind. The bells tolled. Gheorghe eyed the speculating rooks as they cawed in the branches. Night rolled in as clumsily as this lost wanderer.

*

I have never been so far as the church. I don't know my way home from there. The towers are onions – overgrown and big. I don't like onions.

I prayed that God would help me. Furnicuța was gone and I hoped she was praying too. God understands cows as well as Gheorghe. I saw a well in the moonlight and imagined Jesus sitting at it like he did at Jacob's well so long ago. The bucket made a noise in the wind and I was thirsty. The people had chained the bucket to the roof of the well. Why were they so unfriendly and why was it so dark? I sat by the well and waited for the light but it would not come. I looked to the sky but the dawn was nowhere to be seen.

I think I fell asleep. In my dream walks, I saw Jacob digging another well which would be called Gheorghe's well. I was happy. He was so kind to me and had a face like morning. He gave me a cup of water, a hug, and was kindly giving Furnicuța a drink from a shiny silver bucket which they have in story books. I have never seen Jesus but he lives in my heart. I do not like dreams though because you feel nice and happy and then there is nothing but memory.

I woke, and the autumn had appeared with the day. The brown and orange land was misty. There was a noise in the trees. I looked up. A squirrel with a big tail was looking at me. The squirrel was very nice but it wasn't Furnicuța. I missed my friend. She is soft and hard-working. Her eyes are like mine; they are brown and autumn. Her hoofs are good at crunching leaves especially when they're on the floor. I hoped she was safe and that she had found a stream to drink from.

I was very thirsty. I said goodbye to the squirrel and started walking again.

I came to a dark valley and found a stick to help my legs. A good stick is a third leg. But a stick doesn't have knees.

I heard barking. I cried. Three dogs were growling like the noises of Badaceni. The dogs were lions and I did not feel like Daniel. I prayed. The black dog had the grinding teeth of hell. The white dog was silent. The grey dog ran towards me. The dog bit me and I cried and kicked. I cried and kicked. I kicked. God heard my prayers, and the dogs saw a rabbit in the field. They lost interest in Gheorghe and ran after the rabbit. I hope the rabbit was alive but I did not see. I hope Furnicuța is safe from dogs and evil.

Around the time that Gheorghe sat at the soft-stone well and the squirrel meditated in the branch, holding its acorn like an ancient manuscript, Sofia became unsettled like a mother missing her son at twilight. Some of the local boys had received a leaflet with a picture of Gheorghe's face grinning on the front:

MISSING
GHEORGHE
CASA MATEI
SOFIA

Now Gheorghe was not the only man who took his cow to the cowherd every morning. Usually, Sofia's sons would also take their cows. These teenagers had befriended Gheorghe and were truly troubled when they read the leaflet. Unlike their babushka grandmothers, they decided that they would fill the darkness with light.

'Maybe he'll see the lights and be drawn home,' said one of them, hurriedly gathering some timber near the church. The other boys folded their arms, folded their cigarette papers, and stared into the dust.

'I will come as well,' said another.

'And I.'

Another friend, whose wife was on the verge of giving birth, had been troubled by the whole affair and decided to accompany the youths with his grandfather's green lantern.

Within half an hour, the fires roared like ancient beacons and the young men filled the sky with their cries.

*

I was sad and lost. I felt like the man in the Bible who stayed with the pigs. I was hungrier than Jesus in the desert and thirstier than Jonah in the whale. You see, there was plenty of water in the belly but it was salty, and salt water makes men mad. I don't know what it does to women.

I cried for many hours and my ankle was red from dogs' teeth. I found some streams and sat in the waters. It was stinging but I was also able to drink. I could see fires burning in the distance. I like fire and imagined the warmth on my hands. I had cold hands from the water and hoped that Furnicuța was warm. I'm glad she has four legs. I think it is good to have spare legs.

I entered a new village and a woman was sweeping with her broom. She gave me milk and bread. On the table, there was a picture of a man who looked just like me!

When Katya came I was happy with tears. Coming home to *Casa Matei* was heaven. The men from the pasture gate were crying and hugging me like angels. One of them shook his finger at me because he had missed the birth of his child whilst looking for me in the meadows. There was a lot of noise. I kissed Petru, Slava and Grișa and left them for the barn.

Furnicuța was lying down. She looked warm and happy. I gave her a hug and cried waterfalls over her black coat. I gave her favourite foods and sat with her until the moon turned orange again.

Cynan Llwyd

The Humiliation of Basboosa

Runner-Up: Prose

Mohamed woke up sweating. He felt an invisible hand choking his throat; pressing hard and digging deep. His room tasted of harissa and he saw smoke rising from the floorboards.

Then all was calm.

He had dreamt that he was crossing the desert on camelback with his father riding alongside him. They each took turns at storytelling and singing. The ballads for lost lovers, odes to heroes and riotous chants made the sand dance dizzyingly along the dunes. Each melody the same as the previous one, yet different. Hills of golden sand stretched out like a mass of men praying. Rising and falling as one. A carpet of living sand, the whistling of the wind a murmur of prayer. The sun was viciously bright, yet it didn't burn. Mohamed had never felt so comfortable. His father rode next to him; his great black beard shining and his eyes glistening. He looked young and healthy. Mohamed had reached for an orange, peeled it, and the juice cascaded down his throat and his chin. His father roared with laughter at the sight of his son making a mess, before clutching his chest and wincing in pain.

"Father?"

Mohamed heard screaming.

To his right, half buried in the sand, was his mother and his siblings. Screaming, shouting, crying whilst scorpions stung their cheeks.

"Father! Don't die! Don't leave us with only Mohamed! The stupid fool is useless!"

Mohamed turned back to his father who had by now fallen from his camel, slowly disappearing into the golden sand.

*

"Mohamed, please! That will kill you one day, I swear it. I bet your lungs are as black as the Stone," Leila half-pleaded, and half-laughed at her brother who took a long, hard drag of his loose cigarette.

"This won't kill me, Leila," Mohamed gestured to the limp white stick in his hand, "but this will." Mohamed waved his hands in front of him causing ash to fall on the mound of papers spread out on the kitchen table like fallen leaves.

Poverty, Mohamed thought, *poverty will kill me*.

"Don't worry, brother," Leila said, reading her brother's thought. "You will find other work. Have faith!" Leila left her brother in the kitchen. Mohamed sat at the table and thought that his life was a shrinking cigarette; bitter and limp. Its embers dying with every puff.

The house shook, thanks to the onslaught of his Uncle's gut-busting coughing, and Mohamed was reminded of the burden of being the only man able to work in the family. He was young and strong. Not as strong as he wanted to be, but at least he didn't resemble an egret's leg. He read and wrote and counted and wanted to be more than a street fruit vendor. But he was poor. His village education wasn't good enough even for the army. You needed letters before and after your name to get by. Mohamed had none. He was just Mohamed Bouazizi. Twenty-six years old. Chiselled cheekbones and dark brown eyes. Chin built like a pyramid and waves of curls like an elaborate henna pattern. Tarek el-Tayeb Mohamed Bouazizi. Basboosa to his friends. He remembers a proverb he heard an Elder say once. "Because he has so many trades, he is unemployed." He has many dreams, not many trades, our Basboosa. But he is not unemployed, yet.

Mohamed stretched out his arms and lowered his head to the table like he would during prayers at the Mosque. He closed his eyes and saw his father's face again. But not quite. It wasn't the kind and smiling father he saw, but one wearing a disappointed frown.

"Mohamed, get up. You lazy man!" The sharp voice of his dear mother woke him from his daydreaming with an added whack on his back for good measure. "I need my medicine. My sugar levels are as high as Jabel ech Chambi. My throat is like the Sahara and I'm pissing worse than my great uncle did, God rest his soul, and may he climb to the highest levels of Jannah." She picked up a piece of paper from the table and let out a hideous groan like a cow giving birth. "Another rejection? Mohamed, what is the matter with you? Not only is your left ear higher than your right ear, you can't find better paid work. Quick. Quick. Out you go. Go sell your bruised bananas."

Mohamed was led out of the house and from his self-loathing slumber by his mother. She was flapping her arms wildly behind him and showering him with a torrent of abuse. As had happened many times before, Mohamed felt like a dumb goat driven by a demented farmer.

It had been an unremarkable morning. Hot and slow and tasting of petrol. Yellow taxis sped past and honked their horns for no apparent reason. Troops of silver pickup trucks made their way down the potholed street that stretched the length of Sidi Bouzid and their pounding music drowned the laughter of the doves. After giving a family that was poorer than he was a bag of fruits for free, Mohamed promised himself that one day he would buy a silver pickup truck so that he could carry a ton of apples around the city, delivering his goods to offices and schools. Maybe that will catch the attention of a woman, he thought. In the meantime, he would have to make do with his wheelbarrow of fruits.

Mohamed saw her walking down the street towards him. The Terrible Tunisian Tigress. His heart was a stampede of galloping gazelles inside his chest and his legs melted like wax. It was fear rather than love. It was what she represented. Power. Authority. Years of harassment. She was the face of a system that would buy a gold ingot from you in exchange of dirty underwear.

There she is, Mohamed thought. "Look at her," he wanted to shout. "Smell the evil oozing out of her every pore." But all she received as she waltzed down the street were respectable nods and greetings. Why? Everyone knew that the system was corrupt because the system depended on everyone being part of it. The kings and queens and the poor paupers. It was an invisible angel roaming the streets bringing forth life and death. It was a plague and a party in equal measure.

She stood before him, hand on hips, eyes heavy with mascara and a thick smudge of shadow beneath her already dark eyes. She wore her hijab tight so not a single strand of hair was seen. Her Dolce & Gabbana sunglasses crowned her head and the smell of her expensive perfume hung in the air like pollen. Mohamed was aware of the sour taste of his sweat tickling his nostrils.

"Papers," she said. Not a question or a command. A statement? Maybe. Papers. You needed Papers. Your place of birth was known because a Paper said so. Your parents standing in the community was decided because of a Paper. You only existed because a piece of crumpled-up Paper existed. Papers are more important than people it seems. But Mohamed knew that you didn't need any Papers to sell fruit on the streets.

"Sorry?"

"Are you as dumb as you are foul-smelling?" The insult stung like a bee. Mohamed hastily produced the Papers he had on him. The woman snatched them and gave them to her male colleagues who stood behind her. They scanned the words on the Papers and one whispered in her ear.

"You need the appropriate Papers to sell fruit on the street. You should know that, fool," she spat like a venomous snake.

"You should know that I don't need any Papers to sell fruit in the street. You should know that having to provide Papers to earn pennies to cover the debt that you have so kindly bestowed on me, let alone money to earn a living for myself and my family, is against His law. Greed has no religion but itself, so YOU, snouted, trottered, foul Pig, are an Infidel. A blasphemer," Mohamed wanted to scream, but his submissive reply was a slight nod and a hard stare at the dusty ground beneath his feet. A colony of ants made their way towards the wheelbarrow.

The woman made a signal with her hands and the two men stepped forward and took hold of the wheelbarrow.

"Wait," Mohamed pleaded. "What are you doing?"

"No Papers, no selling fruits."

A sizeable crowd had gathered. It was lunch hour and they

22

were happy to be provided with entertainment free of charge. Hungry, the watching crowd ached for drama. Mohamed looked at his audience. He saw brothers from the mosque and mothers who would buy his oranges now feasting on his misfortune. Mohamed hoped that the curtains would be drawn closed on this spectacle and that he could escape to the shadows of the wings. But there they were, awaiting the final act. In desperation, Mohamed struggled with the two men. He shoved one gently, almost politely, and kindly asked the other to stop. He turned toward the woman to plead a final time for them not to confiscate his wheelbarrow.

It happened in a flutter of a wing. As he turned towards the woman, she raised her right hand and slapped him hard across his cheek and the combination was completed by a heavy phlegm expertly aimed from her mouth. He felt it strike his cheek and imagined for a second that a slug was stuck to his face. Before stepping away she whispered in his ear, "They tell me the whores miss your father greatly…"

They led his wheelbarrow away. Shocked, frozen and with his face swelling, he scanned the crowd furiously looking for kindness. Each face he met turned away in humiliation. Not because they felt embarrassed for not stepping in to help but because they felt the utter humiliation Mohamed felt. Slapped in the face … in public … by a woman. The onlookers disembarked, eager to spread the news of what had happened, and Mohamed was left on his own writing tomorrow's reviews. "Humiliating performance", "Man dealt a deadly blow", "How can he recover from THAT?"

He walked the streets like a leper. How quickly words spread in small towns, he thought. No one to call him Basboosa. Spat upon and slapped by a woman clearly made him unclean. Like Moses walking through the Red Sea, the population cleared a path for him that lead to the governor's office. Flustered, sweating, shaking and with dry phlegm adorning his cheek, he demanded to see the governor. The young lady who sat behind the oak desk at reception asked him to sit and wait whilst she phoned the governor's secretary. Mohamed obliged and drummed his fingers on his lap in apprehension. As she spoke on the phone the receptionist could see from the corner of her eye his right leg twitching uncontrollably and the other visitors who were waiting shuffling away from him in fright. She placed the phone back down and Mohamed jumped to his feet like an electric spark.

"Well?" he asked.

"The governor refuses to see you," she replied, apologetically, but before she finished her sentence Mohamed had stormed out of the building.

The dove sits in her nest. Perched high above the street in her silver dress she watches the humans going back and forth. She can't help but laugh at them. It's easier to laugh than cry, she thinks, and nods in agreement with herself. How selfish they are.

After admiring her green and purple necklace, which is shining in the sun, she watches a man running across the road. He goes into the garage. He re-emerges carrying a canister. He slowly walks back across the road but stops in the middle and pours whatever he was carrying over him, washing himself clean in the afternoon traffic. He faces the governor's office, arms open wide like the prophet Christ on the Cross.

"How do you expect me to make a living? Do you hear me? It is finished," the man shouts towards the heavens to no one in particular. Some of the dove's feathered neighbours take off in fright, but this one chooses to stay and watch.

How horrible it must be to be like them, the dove thinks, *to be a bird without wings. And how lovely it is to be a man without sorrow*, she adds.

The smell of petrol has filled the street. The spark from the lighter is lost as the man is engulfed in flames. He runs around like a dog chasing its own tail before falling to his knees. People run towards him, then stop, afraid of what they might see, or too shocked by the devilish smell of burning flesh. An orchestra of screams, shouts and sirens has led to a revolutionary crescendo. People recognised the man. The same people who enjoyed his humiliation are now empowered by his passion. They're chanting his name. Basboosa. Basboosa. Basboosa. They're calling for the world to be turned upside down.

Smoke rises, and the breeze takes it eastward.

Kelly Bishop

Generation Z

We flick through social media like pyromaniacs
wanting to watch the world burn and crumble
under the weight of self hatred.

We put our worth in a number of likes,
warnings that pop up like animatronic
Whack-A-Moles on our screens.

We cross ourselves on our wrists,
The mark of a closed-minded generation.
We leave sleeves rolled up so you can see the pain
caused by middle-aged men with a fetish for people
labelled.

We are cynical because our fathers never loved us.
We need to be noticed because that
is our new currency.

We are apathetic because we feel entitled to be spoon fed
for free.
News straight from the mouth of government,
a spoonful of porridge made with spoiled milk that leaves
    us sick
of politics.

We swallow the sweet saltiness of cum because
    pornography tells us
"That's what women do".
We listen to the teachings of these educational videos that
    leave us ill-informed.
We still believe that women are equal because a law was
    passed,
but men still expect dinner on the table, and children.

We promote products to preteens
for a paycheck.
We multitask but refuse to become masters.

We are private people with private lives
That we live on social media.

We post online for empathy,
drawing on our narcissistic tendencies to quell our
    insecurities that blossom into anxieties.

We expect sympathy.
Cis white lives are reimagined by media's
    heteronormativity.
We expect people to live like us because we have the
    dominant genes.
We are the people you should aspire to be.

We are inspirational in our delusions.
We are entrepreneurial in fulfilling our desires.

We are individualistic because we long for community,
but our introversion leads us down the rabbit hole of
    Tumblr,

behind usernames,
catfish photographs,
exploring self harm and suicide.

We are hyper-aware but refuse to engage because what's the
point when we can change nothing.

We throw ourselves from bridges and cliffs
because we have already been touched by the hand of
death,
cloaking our lives in black,
so that his final embrace will be
blissful.

Laura James-Brownsell

The Day the Earth Died

"The sun giveth, now the sun taketh away," I slur, staring out across the garden. It was hot. Heat slipped into everything, the kind of heat that made you want to collapse somewhere and stay there. It had been like this for five months.

"What the hell you drinking?" my friend Rafael murmurs beside me. I lifted up the beer bottle in my hands, wincing as sun rays bounce off the glass and collide with my eyes.

"Sorry, beer makes me theological. Don't know why I'm drinking this stuff anyway. It's warm."

"It's all we have," Rafael reminds me as I move to toss the bottle away.

"Oh yeah. That's right." There was no more water. A drought had been declared a year ago, but it hadn't been enough. The warnings and the water guards and the sight of children dying of dehydration hadn't been enough. The water had run out four months ago.

"What did you want to do? When you thought about the future, what did you think of?" I ask Rafael.

He tosses back his head and laughs, beads of sweat dribbling down his face. "I wanted to go snowboarding. I wanted to explore the Himalayan mountains and meet the people who lived there. I wanted to get my degree in geopolitics. Make a difference. What about you?"

The trees on the horizon are beginning to light up like

29

motion sensors. We don't have to move, not yet. Probably won't anyway. There's nowhere left to run.

"What did you want to do when you grew up?" Rafael asked, his voice laced with a hint of mirth.

"Not worry. Be happy. Watch history being made." I suppose I've achieved two of those goals, but not in the way that I imagined.

Rafael peers at the growing fire coming towards us. It's moving faster now, the only thing not so beaten down that snail's pace is the only way to go.

"We should probably move. The caves on the beach should be fairly cool," he comments.

"Mmm, assuming we can find a cave long enough." We pick up our things, moving like sloths, sweat pouring down us in waves as we try to urge our bodies to move a bit faster. I can smell the smoke now, tickling my nostrils and slipping into my lungs. We trot out of the house and head for the beach, each breath coming out in a rattling, exhausted gasp. Eventually, we make it and crawl into the nearest cave. It's not long enough, not to protect us from the boiling ocean water.

But it'll do, for now.

"How long do you think we've got left?" I ask Rafael.

"Once we've found a longer cave, days," he murmurs hoarsely.

I guess this is it then. The time to take the final leap into the unknown. There's no point in trying to go on any longer. Not with the world on fire. There's nothing left for us but a painful death by sun or sea. I slowly pull out two bottles of cyanide from the pocket of my trousers and hand one off to Rafael who swallows and refuses to meet my eyes.

"Our father, Who art in heaven, hallowed be Thy name," I whisper to myself. I open the bottle and down the contents.

"Thy kingdom come," – the cyanide burns, I have to lie down – "Thy will be done, on earth as is in Heaven. Give us this day our daily bread and forgive our trespasses" – I can't see Rafael. Panic and pain race through me but I can't get my body to move.

"As we forgive those who trespass against us." I can see Rafael now. He hasn't taken the poison. He's leaving, leaving me. But it's okay. I forgive him. He's always been the optimist. "And lead us not into temptation, but deliver us from evil." I'm not sure if I believe in an afterlife, but anything is better than here. Anything is better than trying to survive the end of the world.

Megan Thomas

None the Wiser

Dominic pulled the knot of his orange tie away from his neck and used the back of its tip to wipe the sweat from his forehead as he made his way to Freshfield Road. He had chosen to start out in Goose Green because he had a friend who lived in the area when they were younger. He'd found that the residents were generally quite community driven, but more importantly, it was a reasonably well-off part of Wigan and a lot of them were elderly. That was the best way to ensure there was somebody at home, according to his dad. His dad had always said that areas like this were the easiest work, and there was no doubt Dominic's dad had enough knowledge and experience to be trusted. He turned left onto Freshfield Road, off Kellbank, towards the cul-de-sac. He decided he would start on the left.

He walked across a small, orderly front lawn, avoiding the empty milk bottles on the doorstep next to a worn-out Welcome Home rug and a soggy copy of *The Daily Mail*. He knocked on the door three times. He'd been practising what he was going to say, constructing his speech with a combination of what was in his handbook's recommendations and what his dad had demonstrated so many times during his childhood. He'd even worn a colourful tie, which his dad said made people feel more comfortable. He heard footsteps behind the door and tightened his tie, straightened his name badge and stretched his shoulders back in a circular motion, taking one last meditative breath before an old woman poked her head around the door. Now was his chance.

"Hello, my name is Elder Taylor and I am a representative of Jesus Christ."

Crushed it, Dominic thought. It was highly uncommon for people to make it through their entire opening sentence on their first try.

"Are you one of them Jehovah people?" asked the woman as she opened the door wider, which Dominic considered a success despite the fact that he was *clearly* not a Jehovah's Witness. He thought after all that Book of Mormon nonsense on the West End, people would at least be able to identify their attire correctly. He remembered the language section of the handbook, which urged you to use 'refined, dignified language' that would 'clearly identify you as a servant of the Lord'. Dominic hated the word servant.

"I am a servant of the Lord, and a missionary of The Church of Jesus Christ of Latter-day Saints."

"Who is it, Martha?" came a voice from a room at the back of the house.

"It's one of them Jehovah people!" she bellowed back. Dominic gritted his teeth and kept his cool, despite his growing unholy frustration. She was still there, which was more than he'd expected.

"I'm of the Mormon church and I wish to share with you some of the wonderful teachings in this book," he said as he pulled out his small, black bible from his jacket pocket and held it up to eye level.

"Martha, tell him to fuck off. I'm pushing play…"

"Excuse him, he gets pissy when EastEnders is on. What did you say your name was, love?"

"My name is Elder Taylor. Could I perhaps join you, and

33

then afterwards share with you the teachings of our Lord and Saviour, Jesus Christ?" Dominic realised this was a long shot, but he thought that perhaps the pressure from inside combined with whatever had kept her from slamming the door in his face in the first place would come to his rescue.

"MARTHA."

"Oh sod it, come in. He'll watch it without me if we don't hurry."

Dominic was riding what he imagined to be the closest thing Mormons got to a high as he walked through the front door into the narrow, beige-carpeted front room. He couldn't believe how much trouble people back at the church had with this kind of thing; everything seemed to be going just to plan. Martha hurried towards the door on their right, shuffling as fast as Dominic imagined was possible in such fluff-covered slippers.

"Martha, who is…?"

"He's a lovely young church man and he's going to watch telly with us and then tell us about Jesus."

"For Christ's sake, Martha…"

"PHIL," Martha cried desperately, nudging her husband while Dominic tried not to laugh. His father was right; old people were definitely the easiest targets. Well, his father would never have referred to them as targets, he was very serious about his life as an elder in the church. He had tried so hard to get Dominic as excited as he was about the Mormon faith, but Dominic thought the idea of spending his life convincing people of something that they were probably correct in mistrusting was a complete waste. They watched the latter half of a very confusing episode, while Dominic eyed the contents of the room. There were no pictures of children or grandchildren, just the couple travelling the world. The mantelpiece above their little fake fireplace was covered in trinkets that had probably been acquired on the photographed travels. There was a small beaded elephant, a wooden sloth hanging from a branch, some intricately detailed plates and a boomerang. Dominic was snapped out of his seated snooping by the sharp drumroll indicating the end of the show, and Phil got up immediately and left the room. Dominic heard the sound of pots clanging and the kettle boiling. Phil was well-trained, it seemed.

"Cuppa?" Martha asked, motioning her willingness to get up off the embroidered throw on their brown sofa to go to the kitchen. Dominic was desperate for a cup, but had to turn down the offer for the sake of maintaining the role. She really did know very little about the Mormon faith, which was useful because she would've known that they usually do this kind of thing in pairs.

"No caffeine for Mormons. But thank you for offering. And thank you for having me in your home, I can tell from the offset that you are the type of loving person who would fit right in with my fellow elders and sisters."

Martha looked oddly smug, like Dominic had just confirmed something she'd thought to be true all her life but nobody had bothered to comment on. She tucked a strand of straw-like grey hair behind her ear, half laughed, half breathed a faux-dismissive "oh" and made a little waving hand movement like there was a fly in front of her. What a sucker, he thought. He had her right where he wanted, though she was admittedly more susceptible than most. Perhaps Phil had something to do with the way she looked drunk on his compliments.

"Oh, but yes, Martha. So hospitable and friendly. You have the potential to worship your way all the way through the ranks in half the time most sisters do." He paused,

35

waiting for a response that didn't come. "Your photographs are lovely. You seem well travelled. How did you and Phil meet?"

"Ah, we met when we were just dopey teenagers. Our parents didn't approve, so we went travelling and left them in the dust. We bonded over our mutual love of food. Though, I must admit, Phil does most of the cooking…" Mid-sentence, she suddenly looked concerned, like she had realised Dominic might be trying to convince her of something devious. "Are you them ones who have lots of wives? Because I know he's a bit of an old grump sometimes but me and Phil aren't looking for any of that funny business."

Dominic laughed, amused by the notion of door-to-door swinging recruitment. Of course that was the element of the faith she had heard about. His laughter, though seemingly reassuring her to some extent, also seemed to disappoint her slightly.

"You sure know your history, Martha. But the church excommunicates anyone practicing polygamy these days. That was discontinued over a century ago, and nobody wants to let us forget it."

Martha laughed charitably whilst fidgeting with a glass turtle on the table next to her, clearly reaching the boundaries of her hospitality. Dominic could see he was running out of time, so he refocussed the conversation.

"I don't wish to disturb you any longer on this lovely evening, might we meet tomorrow for me to further discuss my teachings?"

"Well, actually. I don't mean to offend but I'm not sure I'm interested. I've never been much of a religious person, me." This was the optimum response, because Dominic really couldn't be bothered to start his teachings speech, especially considering he was already inside.

"May I use your rest-room?"

He was directed to the upstairs bathroom. It was more "go up and then it's right in front of you" than a set of directions, so Martha left him to it. He opened the bathroom door and closed it again, feigning an entry. Then he snuck into the main bedroom and started quietly opening cupboards and doors until he found anything of value. He came upon Martha's jewellery box, which he immediately started emptying into his pockets.

His father would be turning in his grave knowing what his son was up to. For years, he had tried to convince his son of the wonders of Jesus Christ and the wonderful things that had happened in Utah all those years ago. But Dominic had steadfastly refused to hear a word about the faith since he was about fifteen. After his mother died, Dominic felt as if he knew for certain that there could be no all-powerful God. Not one with good intentions, at least. Whereas Dominic's father simply became more embedded in the faith, pushing the church's agenda and Dominic to the point where he eventually left home and never got in touch again. Dominic quite liked the parallel of using his father's life teachings to do just the opposite of what those teachings meant to him. His father had spent so much of his life a servant, with doors being slammed in his face. But Dominic had other plans.

*

"Phil, psst. Come back in here. He's upstairs."

"Well, what d'ya know. That was an easy one." Phil came into the room to see Martha quickly and efficiently sharpening her knife. "You're going for the knife? Surely the pills would be easier, Martha. We've just got the carpet cleaned after that television repair man was in."

"Not got much of a choice, he isn't thirsty, is he. I should've pretended it was decaffeinated tea, or offered him some squash or something, but honestly I was just too excited. Have you got the pot ready?"

"And the veggies chopped. Those religious ones always are such suckers, aren't they? So keen to convert people that they'd walk right into a lion's den if it meant reading us a bit of their book." He paused and they both shared a giggle. "Ssh. He's coming back."

Dominic made his way down the stairs and walked back to where he could hear the couple whispering. Dominic was smiling, having completed what he considered to be the first success of a long and prosperous ploy. But Martha and Phil had other plans.

Kathy Chamberlain

As the Vision Fades

Anna doesn't understand exactly what it is that her father does. She's nine and supposed to stay hidden in the kitchen-cum-laundry room at the back. She sits in the nook between the washing machine and the hot, rumbly dryer, waiting for a visitor to arrive. She peeks into the twilit hallway through the gap in the kitchen door.

The women who arrive look at the floor. Some wear headscarves. Others wear their anxiety on their bitten lips and fingernails. The men hand their woollen coats to Anna's father, then march along the corridor to the room. Anna has never been allowed in during a session.

'You've got the special job,' Dad says, tucking a lock of her blonde hair behind her ear.

Between clients, it's her responsibility to 'reset' the room. Anna carries folded purple sheets from the stack on the dryer. Strips the single bed – the only bed in this one-storey building her father inherited through circumstances that remain mysterious. She remakes the bed. Washes the water glass in the browned kitchen sink and refills the jug.

Sometimes a gentleman makes a request: a newspaper, a brandy. She carries the item on the steel tray that came with the building. Knocks twice on the door. When he answers, her father is brief but not unkind. Her mother fell in love with his smile, and Anna wonders whether she will ever get to see it.

It's usually late when they get home, having stopped off at the bakery two streets over. Johnson and sons. She bets her dad wishes he had sons instead, considering. He leaves her outside, then re-emerges with arms full of odds and ends. Half a tiger loaf and some crumbled Welsh cakes. When he carries them up to Isobel with a cup of tea and a much nicer tray, he sets them down on her bedside cabinet and tells her he made them 'fresh this morning'. Every night, his wife pushes herself up against the soft pillows and smiles.

Anna's allowed to climb into the bed with her while her father showers. She has to be careful not to accidentally put her weight on her mother's limbs. When that happens, Isobel winces, and sometimes Dad emerges from the bathroom to evict her. Most nights, though, she is careful, and her mother is serene.

'Anna, cariad. What lovely things did they teach you today?' Anna's never quite sure where she means – school or the business.

She tells her mother things to make her smile. Sometimes they're true.

Isobel cups her cheeks, searches her eyes. Even on days when Dad carries Mam down the narrow staircase and sets her in the rocking chair, buried under blankets. Even then, Anna feels her mother worrying over her as she plays with her wooden train set, or puffs into her recorder, fingers hovering uncertainly.

'Stop watching for signs,' she's heard Dad mutter. 'You'll drive yourself mad wondering.'

Nobody watches Anna during a session. At her bravest, she creep, creep creeps down the hallway, in just her socks, right up to the door. She hears nothing but the ticking of the clock, accompanied by the occasional throat-clearing. Afterwards she might catch a glimpse of an ashen face, but visitors are quick to flee once free.

When Anna's thirteen, the rumours begin. She's alone in the classroom, washing out paint pots when Eleri comes in. Eleri's fifteen and knows everything.

'Your old man,' she begins, tilting her head. 'My dad says he's a fancy man.'

Anna doesn't have a response. Money's tight, she knows, and her father's clothes are anything but fancy. Her silence seems to displease Eleri, who flounces off to try her luck with the girls gathered in the playground.

That night, Anna wants to ask her mother about it, but the urge dissolves in the pool of inarticulate anxiety in her stomach. Instead, she lies on top of the floral bedspread and absorbs Isobel's worries. After the recent election, she's concerned about the business – how can Anna's father keep the bakery going with another five years of austerity? Pastries are a luxury, and Isobel is a burden. She wishes she could give him a hand.

But Anna knows her mother would never support whatever Dad's really doing. If one thing's certain in the murky double life he's dragged Anna into, it's that.

While the schoolyard chatter continues to swirl around her by day, accusing her family of increasingly nefarious acts, Anna becomes bolder at night. One afternoon, a boy she doesn't know spits in her face between classes. That evening, her algebra homework abandoned on top of the dryer, she follows her father to the front door. He waits a moment, fingers on the handle. She thinks, watching the other hand raking through his hair, that he's nervous. Maybe he should be.

The visitor is a young woman with copper curls and a wedding band. She gives Anna a meek smile, and at once Anna feels an affinity with this woman. In the room, Dad coughs, and she understands he is offering her – or perhaps begging she take – a last chance to leave. Anna takes the window seat, and her father presents the woman with a form. The words are familiar, but Anna doesn't understand them. She knows what it is to 'waive all rights', but what is a 'temporal transaction'?

The woman only has one question: 'Will it hurt?' And then she's lying down on the purple sheets, needle in her arm, a thin wire connecting her wrist to the computer. Anna's the one who flinches at the injection, which renders the other woman unconscious.

'I really think you should leave now.' Dad's voice is clipped, which tells her she should stay.

Anna watches the sleeping lady. She's almost bored, bottom numb, when it happens. The woman's mouth opens, and she begins to emit some kind of mist. Her breath comes in faint blue plumes of air. Anna's father opens the ottoman in the corner, and the wispy trail floats over and into it, a continuous flow. After a while, Anna excuses herself, and returns to her homework. Loses herself in simultaneous equations. When the visitor leaves, Dad perches on the washing machine. He's the gentleman who needs a brandy tonight.

'What's that mist?' She's not sure he'll tell her, but they've gone this far.

'It's time.'

Anna shakes her head. 'I don't understand.'

Dad sets the glass down. 'That lady was giving – selling – me a month of her time.'

Perhaps she should be asking how, but Anna cares more about: 'Why?'

'People don't have much money at the moment. You know that.'

'But that didn't take a month.' It's an observation, not a question.

He's not looking at her anymore. 'Well, the month isn't really paid upfront. It comes off … you know. At the end.'

'What do you do with it?'

'I sell it.' As though it's obvious.

All this time, while she's been wondering whether he really is a pimp, or a drug dealer, or some kind of Mafioso. This is what he's been doing. No – what they've been doing. Anna reaches for her coat. It's new for the winter, and now she knows that woman's funeral is going to come one month sooner so that she can be warmer.

For the first time, when she talks to her mother, Anna learns what it means to lie to spare another pain, while a secret gnaws at her belly.

Now that she knows what goes on in the room, her father lets his guard down. One autumn evening, the doorbell rings before he's administered the injection. He disappears to deal with the newcomer, and Anna is left with the same woman from the first session she witnessed. Her curls have lost their shine, and her finger has lost its wedding band. Anna wants to ask her why she does this, what could be worth this, but she doesn't. They chat about how cold it is, and what a pretty scarf Anna's wearing, and how many days there are until Christmas.

That Christmas is Isobel's last. She dies on December 27th, in her bed. It's not the peaceful death that films and platitudes have made Anna expect. Isobel fits and sucks raspy breaths, deaf to the 'love you's that rain down on her amidst tears.

Johnson – and sons – cater for the reception after the funeral. There are more sausage rolls than there are people. Her mother The Invalid had few lasting friendships. Returning from a blissful minute alone in the bathroom, Anna passes the woman with the limp copper curls, and looks away.

The voice in her head is spiteful. 'Karma.'

Anna turns sixteen in the spring. Dad wants her to stay in school.

'It's a very tough world without qualifications,' he tells her, head inside the drum of the broken washing machine. 'School gives you the best chance.'

At what? she wants to ask. School gives her a headache. She's sick of the cliquey girls and the never-ending exams. But school's also where Peter is, and she's falling in love with his bashful grin and floppy fringe.

Peter's the only one who doesn't ask about her father. He walks her to work every afternoon, carrying her daisy-studded satchel, then kisses her goodbye. Anna clings to the memory during the long evenings with Dad. When the blue mist makes its way to the ottoman, she traces her lips with her fingertips.

They keep kissing, and she keeps studying, spending sessions in the window seat with *Jane Eyre*. The woman with the curls is a fan of the book. 'Just a slightly more modern *Beauty and the Beast*, really, isn't it?'

Anna doesn't know. The woman lies back on the bed Anna made that afternoon, and closes her eyes, preferring not to look at the needle – the same routine Anna's watched countless times now. She gives up on her essay. The words are blurry. Instead, Anna watches the woman. As the blue mist rises out of her mouth, her features begin to morph, until Anna is staring at her mother's face.

It isn't the first time she's seen Mam since she died. In a few minutes, she knows, the mirage will disappear. But for now, Isobel's felt slippers rest on the covers, and blonde locks lie on the pillow. Anna runs her fingers through her own hair. It's all anyone says to her since the funeral.

More and more like your mother every day.

As the vision fades, and the copper curls return, Anna wonders how true that will prove to be.

Emily Cotterill

John King (Disambiguation)

A pirate, clutches of politicians and an Irish hurler,
there are seventy-three John Kings listed on Wikipedia.
Some of them were fictional and I don't doubt that
some of them were straight up wonderful but not one
is the one with the name that I know – pinned
onto a Derbyshire infant school and a small museum
on the slope to the wharf of his homeland (open on Sundays
by the public car park, up against the old bottle bank.)
John King, inventor of the mine cage detaching hook,
it's not exactly glamorous but then, what is glamorous
compared to catching and catching and catching
our gene pools. Our same shared history. Lifelines.
The stuff that gave me the same face as my father,
or elsewhere that dark-eyed specifically Welsh beauty.
All those bodies that didn't fall, bones that came to the
    surface,
things that grow in the small worlds of these pit lands
but there's not enough history for an encyclopedia page.

Cara Cullen

Cil-Stone

'I was an old house,' I said quietly
On that hillside farm where a stone was found
Dug heel-deep into the flesh of the earth,
A cil-stone in the cold wind just waiting.

'I was a long house' they say of my time,
Of my long sides that held both beasts and men,
In my two belly chambers snug and dark,
To ruminate in the heart of my chest.

I was old when they named me Cil Oer-Wynt,
Settled in my ways with a back bent,
And slack to the flat of the land,
And the rise of the land, and its breathing.

When they raked off my skin and stone-clad me,
All hardened for another age, creeping
With fire fingers into the back lands,
And a stack of lungs to fume the smoke high.

Armoured I went to war and I grew fat,
Slushing milk white with their eyes and their hair,
But new feet always came running tap-tap,
On my slate face, bare toes and legs and hands.

And I breathed deep with the swallow seasons,
And learnt the sounds of my old throat, and theirs;
A silent voice raised from the cold, east-wind,
In my corner with the same words and names.

A great sadness was sunk into that vale,
Veiled by tears as my grey, stubborn rubble
Was picked at, piece by piece, red carrion
Flown far on a heart string, singing and raw.

Until just my heart was left drowned in place,
And I can still feel it weeping below,
Where swallows once flew, now drifting weeds go,
No flowers even to mark my lost grave.

Here my bones stand uncovered, on strange ground,
And I cannot get warm for the shadow,
And my lungs cannot breathe for the dampness
That followed me, from unnatural water.

Ashleigh Davies

Come Back

My visitor was making breakfast when I came into the kitchen. He was stood at the countertop with no shirt on, dreadlocked hair pulled back into a haphazard bun. He was dissecting a watermelon using a bread knife, eventually carving out a crescent that he laid on a plate. His elbow was a spider web with three spiders trapped inside.

I fixed myself some cereal and sat at the kitchen table. He sat opposite and propped the morning newspaper up using a juice carton. Somewhere in the house a radio was rattling away – a low hum of white noise. I saw that the heat wave was continuing. The early morning sky was shot through with rods of blonde sunlight. The visitor gnashed at the melon. I could hear him crunching down on the beetle-black seeds. It set me on edge a little. I gazed absently at the back of the newspaper where a headline was painted in large cartoon letters.

He had been with me for about a month – renting the spare room. I'd see him at mealtimes occasionally – or lounging by the pool where he could work through a dozen stubby bottles of Pilsner in one sitting. He didn't have much to say and seemed easy with the whole situation. He'd paid his first three months of rent in cash – a bundle of notes that were packed together using an elastic band.

"Any plans for today?" I asked. He smacked his lips and

reclined in the chair, scratching absently at his torso. His skin was dark tan and he carried a bowl of fat low on his stomach that appeared distended in some way.

"Might have some business tonight," he said. There was a vague Caribbean lilt to his voice. I nodded and ate another spoonful of cereal.

"Oh yeah – what kind of business?" I asked – just making conversation. He had never mentioned what it was that he did.

"Business business," he said shortly before grabbing the plate up and tossing it into the sink. I shrugged. He opened the refrigerator and stood there for a short while. This was a habit of his; I had caught him one night, just standing there in front of the opened fridge like a saint bathed in golden light. I must have been staring at him because he addressed me.

"The cold helps with this," he said – and motioned to a scatter of silvered marks that crawled up from his hip to his ribcage.

"Sure," I said and finished my breakfast.

*

He spent most of that day by the pool with his beers. I could never quite tell if he was sleeping or not with his large mirrored aviators over his eyes. Every now and then a spindly arm would extend to grab a bottle, bringing it to his lips for a long draw.

I had a client come around at noon. Her name was Kelly and she had commissioned a series of portraits from me. It was a pretty big deal – my first real gig since finishing an artistry residence at the Metropolitan – four figures. We had met there during an exhibition where she passed me her number. We had dinner a few days later.

I ushered her into the studio and welcomed her to look through some works-in-progress. Most of it was trash – bland pastoral stuff and a handful of nudes that were embarrassing Lucien Freud knock-offs. She gravitated towards one of the smaller easels that was set-up on my bureau. She gestured towards the canvas.

"May I?"

"Yeah sure," I said. "Can I get you something to drink?" I asked. She picked up the canvas and held it close. It was a self-portrait of mine, busy and wild with brushstrokes – not my best work. She noticed the photograph that I used as the model next to the easel – me in a prayer-pose gazing upwards – embarrassingly unoriginal.

"Have you got any vodka?" she asked.

"Yeah I think so – mixer?" I asked. Her eyes were the colour of burnt toast.

"Soda would be great," she answered. I went to fix her drink, dumping a few ice chips into a highball before adding the vodka and soda. I took one of the visitor's beers from the fridge for myself. She was still surveying the canvas when I came back up to the studio. I passed her the drink.

"There's something in this," she said, finally replacing the canvas on the easel. She held the glass against her forehead, a trickle of condensation ran into one of her thinly sculpted eyebrows. I dragged a couple of stools out for us to sit on and we began throwing around some ideas. She seemed fixed on the idea of a triptych. She was one of those talkers with no filter, ideas spilling from her mouth without hesitation.

"How about this?" she said – and pointed back to the self-portrait. An awkward snorting kind of laugh exited my mouth.

"Well it's your call I guess," I said. Her face contorted with an elastic joy. She nodded before throwing the last of her vodka and soda down her throat.

"That would be just fantastic I think." She laid her palm on my arm. I blushed and took a sip from my bottle which had warmed in my hands.

"I don't see why not," I said.

"Well it's settled. Shall we start now?" She stood abruptly.

"I'm thinking the same pose, but three people. Something like this." She took a pallet and a tube of paint, oozing it out before grabbing a brush. She sketched an outline onto each of the empty canvases, they were ruined but I didn't say anything. Her painting was rough, the colour flaring from the edge of the brush like a roman candle. She seemed pleased with the outcome.

I pursed my lips and tried to look pensive. She fished a few ice chips out of the glass and put them into her mouth. She crunched down on them.

"You know I could never have done that as a kid – my teeth were so sensitive," she said. There was a pause where we simply looked at each other for a moment.

"So where would like you like me?" she asked. I fumbled for a moment before gesturing to a corner of the studio where I had a couple of floor lamps set up. I turned them on and dragged over a white backdrop.

"How about this?" I suggested. She poured a heap of ice chips into her mouth before offering the highball to me. I discarded it onto my bureau and brought some supplies over to the easel.

She unbuttoned the top few rows of her satin blouse and pulled it over her head, throwing it over to me. She dragged a clip from her hair and allowed it to fall. She carried her weight high on her hip-bones. I repositioned the lamps and she assumed the prayer-pose. She closed her eyes and I began to sketch out the portrait, trying to ignore the stirring in my stomach.

"You know what would be great," she said, her eyes still closed. "Some music. Something slow," she said.

"Yeah sure," I said and finished a few touches. "Why don't we take a break?" I suggested. She broke from her pose and I went to get the record player.

I fetched back a crate of old vinyl and dumped them onto a stool. She was stood by the window. Her blouse was still at the foot of my easel. I collected it and offered it to her.

"Who's that?" she asked, taking the blouse and holding it in her fist. My visitor was doing lengths in the pool, languid arms pulling him noiselessly through the water.

"Oh, that's just a visitor. Well, half-brother technically." It was difficult to think of him that way. We had never met before he came to stay but my mother had persuaded me to put him up. The official story was that he had been in the army, served a few tours. The unofficial truth was that he had served time. I didn't need to know any more than that.

Kelly was practically draped over the sill. She thrust a couple of fingers between her lips and whistled down at him. The noise was shrill. She waved her blouse like a flag. He eased to a stop and flipped a tress of dreadlocks from out of his face. He looked up through my mother's eyes.

"Can you come up here for a second?" she asked. He dragged himself out of the pool, shedding a blanket of water and swiped a pilsner from next to his sun lounger.

"What's up?" he asked, more to me than Kelly.

"I need to get a better look at you," she said. I laid a hand gently on her arm and tried to lever her away from the window.

"Look, he's busy. This isn't really his thing," I said, trying to keep my voice low.

"He's not busy, he's got all the time in the world."

She wasn't moving so I left her at the window and went back to the pile of recent paintings I had made. I shuffled through them. She babbled to him at the window with her high-pitched voice.

"Here, how about this," I called, holding one of my better portraits up in the air. She dismissed me with a wave and continued to speak to my half-brother. I swore under my breath and drank the rest of my bottle of Pilsner in one gulp, spilling some into the stubble on my chin.

She turned to me, face joyous as a child.

"He's on his way," she said.

*

It turned out she had offered him some money to pose for the third portrait. He skulked around the studio for a while. They flirted and she asked for another vodka and soda. There was music playing when I came back; some obscure rock and roll foot stomper. She was pressed against the wall, her body mostly obscured by his as he kissed her hard on the lips. Her one hand was pulling on the back of his neck, the other searching the stone-wall behind her. I felt awkward and embarrassed, calling to alert her that her drink had arrived. There was a moan of acknowledgement.

I didn't really know what to do so I took a sketch-pad and started tracing the scene they were making. My stomach was lurching worse than it had been before. Her blouse was back on the floor and I tried to concentrate on the page. The music ran beneath everything.

They stopped a while later and he walked over to me, staring absently and scratching at his scarred stomach.

He took Kelly's glass and swigged down the contents, the ice chips clattered into his teeth. He leaned over and viewed my sketch upside down. He grunted and put the glass back down on the bureau.

"I need to go see about something," he announced, and disappeared back downstairs.

Kelly put her blouse back on, liquid satin falling over her shoulders. There was blood in her cheeks. I heard the engine of his car crack from out the window and it pulled away. The light was falling, the studio had filled with clammy summer air that had poured in throughout the day.

"I'm not sure we should let him drive," I said uselessly. I was talking to a different person – she was now distant and aloof, tottering around the studio. She took the glass that he had drained and began crunching down on the ice chips that were left.

"I should be leaving," she said.

*

The phone woke me up during the night. I had fallen asleep in an arm-chair in the living room. I took the call, immersed in synthetic light from the television. My mother's voice was panicked and breathless. I tried to decipher what she was saying but the words were too quick and jumbled – punctuated by looping patois.

"Slow down, mum, what is it – what's happened?" I asked. I was already in the kitchen, the phone wedged between my ear and chin. I was leafing through the mesh of coats and jackets on the back of the door.

"Is he back there?" she asked. I peered through the night towards the driveway.

"No," I answered. I could hear scrambling in the background of the call; there was a baby crying, exclamations of some sort, the slamming of doors. She spoke again in a machine-gun trill of alarm.

"What did he do?" I asked, still surveying the driveway for any sign of his car. The dishes from breakfast were festering in the sink. A bowling alley of empty pilsner bottles were assembled next to the lounger. Frail strands of starlight kissed the water in the swimming pool, the surface was still and taut as a tarp.

"He was here – asking to see the kid. I thought you were looking after him?" she said in an accusing manner. The driveway was split by headlights.

"He's here, mum," I had to shout over her manic protestations. "Mum, I've got it, I'll speak to him." I killed the phone. The engine of his car died and the driveway was again plunged into darkness. He must have sat there for a few minutes before coming back in. He swayed a little, choosing not to acknowledge me. He made a beeline for the refrigerator, opening it and standing in the light. He pulled up the vest he had been wearing and exposed his braided scars to the cool atmosphere that radiated from the fridge.

"Here," I said. I dispensed some ice chips into a towel and beckoned him to the kitchen table where he reluctantly sat down. I pressed the cold towel against his stomach. His eyelids were low and there were scrapes over his knuckles.

"We need to talk," I said.

"Not now." There was a bitterness in his mouth. I nodded and we sat like that for a while in silence.

"That was some shit you pulled earlier," I said, gesturing towards the stairway to the studio. We both cracked a smile at that. We had never really known each other but in that moment it felt like we had been brothers all our lives. The art of discarding shame; we each had our reasons to harbour some. He cackled a little and then gave a long sigh. He shifted the towel and the ice chips clacked against each other. A small disc of water had pooled on the floor beneath his seat. A purpled sunrise threatened the horizon.

"She's not coming back you know," I told him, but I guess he already knew that.

Moon Landing, 1969

He emerges from the amniotic
safety of the shuttle vestibule
into total interstellar darkness.

His costume – more deep sea
than deep field – mirror faced,
rendering space in high definition,

collapsing several billion lightyears
into a visor the size of a polaroid
jutting from the mouth of a camera.

America sits next to the wireless –
singing its hope into the airwaves,
waiting on a moon-bounce response.

Wishing on a turn of the earth
to take us out of the black
and into the blue.

Night Drive

Total interstellar darkness
until the turn of key, kiss of life,
brings the engine up, vomiting fumes;
headlights can only break so far

into the darkness of lanes, monochrome
carousels of gorse, mulberry, blackthorn,
strobe your vision above the smooth
arc of a dashboard needle.

Until the crash, shunt and brake,
swell and diminish of your shirt-front.

Engine grille smashed like the nose
of a prize-fighter. Torchlight lands on
the body of a fox, a recoil of fur
perched on a plate of swelling mahogany.

Panic subsides and the body is swarmed
in a foil blanket, like a fresh caught trout.
only then can you feel the heartbeat, rocking
like a life buoy on some vast Atlantic.

To this you feel obliged to embrace the fox
in a lover's grip, sing a lullaby whilst
your butcher's arm takes neck and muzzle;
fillets the soul, clean from the bones.

Taylor Edmonds

Thanksgiving

Your mother places your father
at the centre of the dining table,
resting on a silver platter
with limbs folded into one another,
mouth full of browned apple,
layer of crispness to the skin.

She invites you to take a leg
and leave the fat, swell of the middle
for her. She wants the juiciest of flesh.
She has been starving herself for three days,
is wearing her best Sunday dress,
pearl necklace draped around her neck.

She holds the rough of her palm
to her heart when saying Grace,
eyes closed, thanking God
for health, food, happiness.
Sit, she tells you, *now we feast.*

Your mother smiles
with a chunk of meat between her teeth.
Take a piece between your fingers,
warm against skin, thick sliver of grease
trailing down towards wrist.

Your mother proposes a toast,
red wine stain around her lips.

Aaron Farrell

Growing Up Hill

I must address the postcode of youth
with all its rigid adornments
the arena was just a town and
a world atop a hill
Until Mam came home with a car
and the dual carriageways awaited
to distant Llansamlet and Llanelli
but that was a travesty against the Hill
unlike Hotel California
we didn't check in, let alone, check out
departure was sinful
toward Gods in tracksuits
throwing fireworks like thunderbolts
toppling caravans like trees
hiding truth like treasures
seeking sex like sailors
deflecting abuse like umbrellas
suckling Townhill's virile bite-marked teat
Paradise Park isn't ironic
not to the feet and the ball kicked along the pavement
punctuated in phlegm and chewed gum
spat out before the forgotten first kiss
it was my first foray
into words that don't represent
dictionary definition but become

mirages of meaning to sand-grain thirst
an interpretation of communal camaraderie
leaving no clan behind
every boy and girl gazes far down
without Pant-y-Celyn altitude sickness
upon Swansea Bay's crescent curve
the contemptuous smile inviting
hissing can parties
and vigils for virginities

All anger at all else
Trespassers will be got
By the TMB and its severely syllabic chant
Foreigners from Mount Pleasant
Aliens from Tycoch
Social pariahs sent home without peace
Dog yelp screech, from the delivery of a steel boot
Sunday school educated us in free sandwiches
the Phoenix centred our pitches
we boxed at the Gwent

Purple eyes stormy with rain
worn as a badge of dishonour
everyone knows what happened on the roundabout
the only thing faster than the joyrides
is the gossip between Abdul's and the Top Shops

So where did I fit?
I didn't, although I tried, mush
amidst my skateboarding on the ramps
used as slippy-slides and kindling
I smashed windows in a stone fight
amidst my learning of Kung-Fu

used as self-defense to 'fat cunt' hostilities
I went too far in attacking a bully
amidst my working at Youth Club
used as a springboard for cultural insight
I detested pat-on-the-back politics
my missing ingredient in a working-class stew
was conformity
however quietly I rejected a schoolyard smoke
or fervently denied a drunken quarry poke
I did not try to fit in
for I was without the ability
to not dream in cinematic Sci-Fi
a fighter's chance, a writer's dance
and the books, the games, the comics, the films,
the distant allure of art far-flung from
five-a-side syntax
all sustained a hunger for another world

I left for American dreams
told by the men leading craned-neck boys
that nothing will change
with hands down the pants
for warmth, if not romance
and upon my return
clad in the dust of heterogenous handshakes
I was not asked how the world was
only told what I did not miss
shagging, jobs lost, enemies found
bets won, bets lost, and nights down town
tethered to the Hill and its rhetoric

Gay faggot ponce pussy
for writing a poem

about being you
which is not this
this could only be written
from passing over in excommunication
sick of home, the plan was hatched
escaped prisoner desperation
without a Cool Hand but a scrimshank redemption
I fled and was not mourned for my pretentious ways
transient rider of terrorist shores
banished les enfant terrible
enabled to rove and roam
with a hardened heart on tattooed sleeve
by a Town on a Hill, I still grieve.

Seeds of Sin

Witch hunts have naught to do with witches.

*

Sitting with folded legs clad in thick tights of weathered wool, Gaia tickled the green hair of the carrots buried beneath the damp soil. The garden spanned from Father's thatched house to the humungous density of Blaidd Wood. Gaia swooshed her wand against the carrot leaves, making rain from dew. Along the wattle fence that enclosed Gaia, her reveries and her thriving vegetables, sat all manner of birds conversing in songs that were sugar to her ears. Thoughts of sugar led her mind to cross a bridge to memories of honey.

*

Father bought Gaia a jar of honey at the markets to gift her a fortuitous birthday. The Bee-Lady patted Gaia's pink cheeks as she handed over the jar of honey. Gaia thought the Lady's hands to be softer than down feathers and discussed as much with Father on the journey home.

The village behind them was blanketed in shadow but the rocky path ahead cutting through fields and forest was paved in mystical pink. Clouds were scratched into the sky like raw scars. This natural world was proof enough to Gaia that magic existed. The jar of honey bounced in her lap as the cart rolled over a rock and she was brought back to Father beside her, reins in hand.

"The Bee-Lady said she bathes in honey once a year to treat her skin. Were Mother's hands that soft?" Gaia's fleshy features were in awe.

Father's sullen face loosened into a serene smile. "This harsh world was a softer one for your mother's skin. Her touch is your touch. She held you in her grasp until the moment she faded away, passing through you to get to the Gate of the Gods."

Though the cart rocked as Blackie whinnied and cantered along, Father was unshakeable in reminiscence. "That's why our harvests are bountiful where the Griff's are not. Your Mother was the talk of Pridd Dol during our first harvest. The vegetables grew fat for her. Now, she's tending to the Garden of Gods."

Gaia nibbled her lip for a second and then blurted her truth forward.

"What makes your Gods real but those from mythology make-believe? When did the old Gods stop tormenting the strong boy facing immortal trials, and the new Gods start making plagues that kill villages? I'm real. Honey is real. But I think Gods are just stories."

"Gaia, you may believe whatever you like but you must mind your tongue." Blackie neighed in agreement and Gaia poked her tongue out at him. She felt Father's stony gaze as if he were *Meydoosa*.

"People don't want your winter snow at their summer feast. Those of unfaltering piety are as paranoid as the worm at dawn. Be careful with words."

*

Gaia shook off the tart-tasting recollection and became aware of the wintry reality paling against the sundown memory.

Tripping over her feet as she stood, Gaia accepted the garden's challenge. She hopped the carrots, skipped over the rows of beans and ran under the scarecrow's arm to arrive at the fence in a fluster. Seemingly immovable on their perched stage, the birds did change their melody in reaction to Gaia's presence. From the pocket of her apron, Gaia scooped a palmful of seed she'd stolen from the shed. Finches, tits, jays, wrens and robins danced in their plumage. Gaia threw the seeds and they scattered on the unkempt grass outside her garden. A chaffinch nabbed a sunflower seed mid-air. Gaia giggled and applauded before leaning over the fence on her tipping toes to observe the collection of feasting friends.

Beside the hopping, pecking and flapping, amongst fallen pieces of thatch, sat a pale broken egg. Half the size of a chicken egg Gaia would crack over a heated pan. She scampered through her garden and out of the gate at the front of the land. She'd learned some time ago not to climb the fence. It was quite feeble in supporting the low hurdles of a young girl bounding great distances in her mind.

The birds pecked contentedly, taking no notice as Gaia approached to inspect the egg. They trusted her. She wrapped gentle fingers around the soft shell, placed it in her palm and peered into the crack. A featherless dead chick. Pink and wrinkled and sad.

"Why is birth so hard? If it's not the mother, it's the child." Though the birds were audience enough, Gaia's soliloquy was scored by the dance of the woods in a sudden high wind. A pitched voice of disagreement from beyond her house failed to defeat the whistling and swooshing. The neighbours,

67

Sioned and John Griff, had four boisterous sons. Sioned was fierce in telling the boys what was right and what was wrong so noise from their land was as natural as smoke from fire. Undeterred in her musings, Gaia's eyes the colour of oceans she'd never see, scanned the immense forest, the white sky, the swaying fields, the distant hills.

"I hope we never hurt you." The landscape appreciated her nobility.

A sharp scream ripped her from her ideals. It was not the cry of a frustrated mother but a fearful one. The birds took to the air in a concert of slapping wings. Had John pitchforked his foot again? Gaia wondered. She gulped hard but curiosity filled her legs.

Two men in crimson leather armour stood over a floored, bloody-nosed Sioned and a petrified John cowering next to her. Gaia halted, kicking over a rake that was leant against the fence as she did so. The soldiers rounded on their heels, giving their backs to the Griffs and their attention to Gaia. The soldier's helmets were in the pocket of their curled arms. Accusatory lines from their irksome grins made Gaia's stomach plummet.

"Oi, girl! Is your name Gaia?" one of the soldiers asked in a voice that dripped with slime.

Gaia was alone. The birds had taken to the safety of the sky. Father was selling seed in town. Sioned and John, who'd check on Gaia in Father's absence, were in no fit state. She didn't answer. She couldn't.

"We have word that you're a Witch, little girl. And Witches must face judgment."

"Fucking idiot, Rodney. We weren't to be saying the word, 'Witch'. Captain doesn't want a fuss until she's proven guilty."

"There's only the Griffs around, Dai. They'll keep a secret.

Lest one of their boys be a sceptic to our great Faith." They smiled, though Gaia found nothing in their words to smile about. They began to approach Gaia, crossing the gloopy cart track separating the Griff's land and Father's.

"I ... I ... I'm not a Witch. I promise," Gaia whispered. Her voice quaking as much as her body.

"And I didn't punch a wench so hard last night she lost two teeth. I promise," retorted Rodney before he and Dai began cackling. Gaia thought they sounded like the Witches.

Rodney and Dai encroached on Gaia as she backed into the wooded wall of her home. Dai placed a mailed arm on Gaia's shoulder, letting her feel its weight, his power. Rodney unravelled a binding rope. Gaia didn't know what else to do but unsheathe her wand. She knew how fearful folks were of their beliefs.

Demons command more respect than angels. Gran's gravel voice resonated in Gaia's mind.

Dai hopped back like a skittish lamb as his scarred chin trembled.

Rodney stood terrified, frozen inside a moment where a girl pointing a wand meant anything was possible. Even magic. But like all moments of multitudinous possibility, its current passed down one of the multiple streams in the river. This stream was one where magic didn't come from decorated twigs, and men's fists knocked little girls unconscious.

Another single scream from Sioned's throat plumed into the bitter air as Gaia was pounded into the cold compacted ground.

*

A choir of harsh screams split her ears as she battled to open her eyes. The muted light burned in her mind, but she needed to understand.

Maes Castell Square was bustling with common folk that had eaten vegetables Gaia had cultivated. Yet they screamed in disdain at her purported witchcraft. A wand was proof enough for the Senior Arbiter that she practised dangerous forms of Mancy as a Witch.

Gaia was being dragged by her arms through the screaming square. A wooden monolith stood amongst a bed of dry brush. The thumping of her headache was mere whimsy to the coagulating fear in Gaia's heart. For she knew the stories of what happened to Witches.

Thoughts of her skin crackling like pork made Gaia retch bile down her apron. The guards didn't notice. Gaia's feet left tiny trenches in the mushy brown ground which absorbed one of her slippers.

How could she be tending her garden in one instant and in the next, be dragged toward her death as a Witch? The reality didn't seem real to her. One person could claim something against another, causing their life to fester into a nightmare in the flap of a finch's wing. And she was helpless to it. Physically and mentally. What could a little girl say to change the mind of men?

She screamed and kicked and cried as the crimson guards that weren't Rodney and Dai stopped for a moment. Their thick bearded faces were incapable of pity. Her struggling changed nothing.

Gaia retched once more as she was lifted over the threshold of the pyre boundary. Nothing came out but an unheard whimper. She was heaved up onto the platform,

70

placed on the foothold and bound to the pyre with tugs of indignant strength. Words came from the Arbiter's mouth as he cited a book so large it could only contain religion. Gaia's eyes focussed on the heavy white sky looming over the town. Her eyes prayed for the sky to take her. She'd never say a bad word against the Gods if they'd help her now.

A roar of ignition snatched Gaia's attention away from the cumbersome clouds and invisible Gods. A torch had been lit and its resonance clawed at her although it was still in the hand of a man in black. Gaia raged against the rope that bound her. She wanted to sprint away with every grain of exertion, toward Father's home, which she realised was a heaven in the hell of humanity. The rope loosened on her last tug but the flames rose from the torches prod, causing mayhem amongst the flammable death of autumnal flora like a starved wolf in a sheep pen.

For a moment, her bare left foot tingled the way it would when Father tickled it with his wiry grey-black stubble. Then her sheepskin leggings caught alight and she was unable to cling to posterity as violent heat ravaged her pliant skin.

Snowflakes began to fall. They were too few to combat the flames that spearheaded into silver smoke. Gaia's howl of agony silenced the crowds, awakening them to the true horror they had enabled and now, were witness to.

The searing external pain was beginning to abate as Gaia's nerves burnt away yet fire continued to violate her mouth, throat and lungs. The flames had eaten the rope around her wrists, causing her to flop from the pyre, down into the fire bed and roll into the short fence housing the cleansing crucifixion. Gaia was no longer Gaia, but a scalded black body flecked with raw pink, flailing to its feet and raging against the air. Before slumping to its knees in finality.

A guttural wail from a man sprinting toward the charred body struck like a bell.

"That's my daughter!"

Gaia's father was sickly pale though his face showed all the terror of existence. He collapsed to his knees, mirroring the smouldering corpse of the child he'd created in love and raised in joy.

Wrapping his arms around her wanting to feel the warmth of her spirit, he instead endured the heat of her crime. That, of a little girl defying the conventions of Gods and Men with imagination.

Eluned Gramich

After the Stag

Maisie was standing in the kitchen, waiting for the kettle to boil. The kitchen was unusually clean; she had spent the last thirty minutes wiping the counter with a damp cloth while listening to Owen's sobs from the other room. She hadn't been allowed to console him yet. She was hoping he would call her eventually, but his best friend phoned instead.

Owen cleared his throat. "Hey, Nikhil. Yeah, I just told her now."

She couldn't hear everything her fiancé was saying. He was speaking softly after all that crying. The door to their living room was ajar, and half a phrase slipped out here and there. A few times she heard, "I know, I know" and "You're right, yeah."

Owen had two best friends: Nikhil and Jonny. She got on well with them both. Sweet lads from Owen's childhood; their mothers had grown up together. When he first introduced Maisie to his Mam, Nikhil and Jonny's mothers had been there too, drinking rosé on the beige three-seater, joking that she needed the approval of all three of them to go out with one of their sons. They had meant it nicely.

Maisie hung the tea towel on the oven door to dry. It was winter. Black outside, and barely five o'clock. The only thing she saw through the window was her reflection: blonde hair scraped back into a bun, her face pale, which made the

73

blusher she'd put on earlier appear garish, like two purple bruises. Normally, Maisie took pleasure in seeing her reflection, but tonight she averted her gaze, looking down at her hands where the engagement ring looked cold and blunt under the kitchen light.

In the oven was a game pie she'd spent the afternoon making, something 'traditional' for her fiancé after the trip to Hamburg with the boys. The *Guardian* recipe was still open on the iPad, propped up against the microwave. She took the plates out of the cupboard and arranged them on the little dining table by the front door. The flat was small – one bedroom, bathroom, living-room and a kitchen-dining area – hardly bigger than the changing rooms at the leisure centre. But it was theirs. They'd bought it together two years ago; shared the mortgage and the insurance. It was the most expensive thing they had ever bought. His Mam had no money, so it was Maisie's parents who helped them with the deposit.

She waited, listening. It was so quiet that she thought she could hear him breathing in the other room.

"Baby, are you alright?"

A creak from the sofa. Silence.

She stood outside the living room holding a bottle of red wine, wondering whether she should enter or not. Her hand was trembling. The situation was ridiculous. Why was she afraid? Afraid of Owen? *Her* Owen?

She whipped off the cap and poured two glasses.

"Baby," she said, pushing open the door. "I've got you a drink."

The blinds were still up, which meant that next-door could peer inside from across the alleyway. She put the glasses down and drew the blinds, before tidying up a little: there was a cushion on the floor for some reason, and the remote control had ended up in the far corner. Had he thrown it earlier? She couldn't remember.

Owen was sprawled on the low, grey sofa. He didn't acknowledge her, but she felt his eyes on her back as she picked up the remote and replaced it on the coffee table.

"Was that Nikhil calling?"

Owen stared sullenly at the carpet. He looked rough, of course, like anyone would after a bout of crying. His cheeks were puffy, wavy hair all over the place, his clothes crumpled after the flight, and there was an odd, sour smell in the room – he'd probably had a few beers on the plane.

"Do you want me to put your stuff in the wash?" she went on, pointing at the carry-on suitcase abandoned by the door.

"Just leave it." His voice was different with her than it had been with Nikhil: hard, detached.

"I made dinner."

Owen wiped his nose on the back of his hand. She hovered, wary of him, knowing she couldn't touch him yet, but wanting to all the same. Outside, she heard the family next-door, stamping up the steps. The girls sometimes stayed with them in the evenings when their parents were out. Owen would lie with them on the living room floor, playing Go Fish. She'd told him, *You're so good with the girls*, and he smiled: *Got to start practising at some point.*

Owen was still staring ahead, his expression closed. It was difficult for her: trying to pick the right moment, the moment he'd give up being angry: go soft and soppy again, let her put her arms around him. It was almost unbearable, waiting for him to give in. She wanted to get on with the evening she had planned. They were supposed to have gone to bed together and he was going to tell her everything about the stag do, the crazy things Nikhil had planned, Jonny's attempts at womanising, the fall-outs and the makings-ups. Then she would have told him about her night with the girls – the West-End show that had cost a fortune but ended up being a bit naff, the seven cocktails the girls made her drink, and how she'd lost her sequin jacket in a club cloakroom. Maisie had the pictures all lined up on the iPad. After that, they were supposed to eat the game pie, drink a bottle of red, watch television cwtched up together. He was supposed to fall in love all over again; to remember how much better it was to be with her than the lads.

"The pie's been in the oven for five hours. If you want some."

She noticed there was a thin stain along the shin of his jeans that resembled blood.

"I'll put some on a plate for you, shall I?"

He didn't even look at her.

She left. Everything was so prettily laid out in the dining room. The kitchen smelled good, much better than the stuffy living room with that stale, traveller air. She took the casserole dish out and placed it on the stove; spooned out a big helping onto the dishes her Mum had gifted them when they'd moved in together.

"I don't know if I put enough salt on it," she said, holding the plate like a peace-offering. "Do you want to eat it here?"

"Jesus Christ." He leaned forward, put his head in his hands. "How can you even think about food now?"

"Just taste it. Go on." She crouched down, holding it out to him as if he were a child. "Go on. I swear you'll like it."

He slapped the fork out of her hand. It came as such a shock that she dropped the plate. The pie landed with a wet thud on the carpet, sending a brown streak of gravy across the beige rug.

"What the hell, Owen!"

It was her turn to get upset. She felt the tears rush to her eyes.

She picked up the upturned dish but, somehow, she did not have enough energy to scoop up the rest of it. The smell of simmering kidney, so delicious in the kitchen, now turned sickly and metallic. She sank to the floor. Owen, on the other hand, was standing with his hands on his hips, facing away from her.

"Can you please stop being like this?"

Owen laughed unpleasantly. "You know this is your fault."

"I said I'm sorry. I've said it a *thousand* times."

He shook his head.

"I don't know what else to do. What should I do?"

"If you don't know then I definitely don't have a fucking clue."

Maisie winced, hearing Owen swear like that. He would never have said 'fucking' in front of her before. In front of his friends, maybe, but not her. She was his *princess*. She almost said it out loud: *Aren't I your princess anymore?* Real tears welled up then, thinking about how it had been in the beginning. How they'd met at Jonny's birthday in the Uplands years ago. How she'd stayed up all night just to be close to him, following him from party to party, until he'd asked for her number and she'd said no just to keep him guessing.

In those days, he'd worn tracksuit bottoms, a Wales rugby shirt and trainers that were falling apart. He was nineteen, first year in college, while she was two years younger, just scraping by at school, not taking it all that seriously. Only she'd taken *him* seriously. Her college boy. He'd been so handsome – still *was* handsome – with those freckles across his nose, that light hair flopping over his eyes and his sweet, knowing grin. He'd made her take off her clothes at Mumbles and they'd gone into the water together, holding each other to ward off the cold.

"Baby! Baby, listen," she said. She was crying quite freely now. Tears dropping into the pool of still-warm food on the carpet. "Listen, it'll be okay."

"Don't you start."

"You know it was a mistake."

"No, it wasn't." He had this strange way of talking suddenly: this cool, far-away voice, while she felt herself giving in, falling apart.

"I won't do it again. I won't. Not ever."

"I don't care if you do."

"We have to be sensible. It's happening in two weeks." For some reason, she got stuck on the word 'wedding'.

"No, it's not."

"*Of course* it is. *Of course* it has to happen."

He shook his head.

She saw her parents, then. She pictured them so vividly that it was if they were in the room, sitting on either side of Owen. Her mother had paid for the venue; her father for the food. They had saved for it; they had borrowed money for it.

"Don't be ridiculous," she told him.

"You'll have to tell them."

"No."

He nodded solemnly. "Either you or Jonny."

"We love each other. We're getting… getting *married*. After this, we can move away. Go anywhere you like. Go to Canada or America. Anything. We can leave this all behind us. Like it never happened. We can turn over a new… a *new leaf*."

Owen stood very still, as if he were considering her words. There were deep creases in his shirt from the journey, and a dark well in the small of his back where the sweat had dried.

"Don't you love me?"

He'd arrived late, around four. He'd come out with it almost as soon as he walked in. Jonny had drunk too much, ended up bragging to one of the others that he'd got with Maisie a few times. More than a few. In a way, it had been a surprise to Maisie to learn that Owen had not known about it. She'd assumed that Owen had known but had decided to ignore it for fear of losing her. Well, it turned out he hadn't known at all. No one had. Not even Nikhil.

"This is a mess," Owen muttered, running his hand through his hair. He returned to the sofa; chose to sit a little nearer to her. Her heart beat faster, hopeful.

They had gone through the times in more detail: when, how, why. She hardly remembered herself. She'd been twenty-two and stupid that first night, and when you sleep with someone once it's easy to fall into it again, like a routine. It's true that Jonny came over whenever Owen was away for a match or for work, but Jonny was a kind of replacement, really. She had tried to explain this, but it hadn't worked. Owen wanted to know, *What does he have that I don't?* She said, *Nothing. Then why?* He'd asked, and she just shook her head, as if there were some deep mystery to it that he wouldn't understand.

"Just be honest with me, Maisie."

Honest? She could have said, *Because he's good in bed.* But she didn't of course.

They'd been through it all, and she was exhausted, famished. Her head felt heavy, as did her whole body, and she let herself spread out on the floor, one arm on the sofa near Owen's lap.

"You'll have to tell them both. My parents and yours."

"The wedding cost sixteen thousand pounds. You know we won't get the money back."

Owen laughed again.

"You have to forgive me," she said, which sounded like a line from television. But there it was: purposeful, heartfelt.

Owen moved his arm so that it touched hers. He squeezed her hand. "Come here," he said.

She did as she was told. Her body felt cumbersome and unresponsive. She clambered onto the sofa where he continued to hold hand. She laid her head on his shoulder and waited for him to put his arm around her.

"It'll be alright," she whispered into his ear, ignoring that sour smell of sweat and beer to be close to him.

"It's best if you call your parents first. Then my Mam," he said.

She started to cry on his shoulder. The sobs were coming from deep inside her chest; she hadn't sobbed like this since she was a child. Owen put his arm around her, kissed the top of her head.

It'll be alright, she thought.

Then he pulled away, patting her back perfunctorily, as though he were consoling one of the girls next door. She thought he was about to look at her, properly this time. Instead, he picked up the suitcase and left the room.

"Baby, wait. Where are you going?"

He was fiddling with the front door, pulling at the catch. "Baby," she was saying, only she was crying so much, the word came out like a wail. "*Don't.*"

"Tomorrow," he said, not looking at her. "Okay? I'll see you tomorrow."

He closed the door. She listened for a while: the sound of his footsteps on the stairs, the suitcase banging against his leg. She hadn't asked where he'd got that stain from, the one that looked like blood on his leg. That was alright. She could ask him tomorrow. She would see him tomorrow. When she'd calmed down, she picked up the cloth from the kitchen counter and stuck it under the tap. She thought it was a shame that he hadn't left the suitcase here, so she could run the clothes through the wash. But it was alright. She would do it next time. Make it up to him. Everything would be alright tomorrow.

She wrung out the cloth. Then went to wipe the game pie from the living room carpet, taking off the ring before she did so.

Emily Green

Good Luck in those Pebbledash Houses

It wasn't long after we first moved that I noticed how Mum didn't lock the front door like she had done in our old house. She usually kept a set of keys in her handbag, tangled up in old receipts and sweet wrappers. But at night, she put them back in the lock and pushed down on the stiff handle. She said it was to make sure nobody could get in while we were sleeping. During the first couple of weeks, our new neighbours tapped on the letterbox to announce their arrival and let themselves in. They'd walk straight through our kitchen and hand my mum cakes with raisins in them that looked like fat flies, while the men went over to shake my father's hand. I'd sit at the dining table, the same one we'd had in our old house, and tried to understand the sounds the new voices made. I'd got into trouble just before we moved, for writing notes on sticky-backed paper to the woman that lived across the road from the school, who always came over at lunchtime. I fixed the sheets to the railings with stolen blu-tac, but the dinner ladies took them down and told me that I shouldn't speak to strangers. Yet now here they were, standing in our new kitchen.

Everyone else in the village still called it The Doctors' House, including the handful of people who lived on our street, but I think that's what helped us to eventually settle in. Our loose association with the doctors who had once owned our new home meant that even though we weren't like the rest of the village, we had been approved, by the type of people that can sign the back of your passport photograph and monitor your blood sugar levels. There weren't many of these types of people in the village. I'd once overheard our next-door neighbour tell my mum that everyone had been stuck in limbo since the mines had closed. I'd recognised the word from watching people play it once at a school disco. The teachers held a plastic stick above the girls in my year, who contorted their pre-pubescent bodies into shapes I never could, while the boys surrounded them, taking off sweaty vests and beating their chests. The neighbour was telling my mum that her boys would never have the opportunities that their grandfathers did down in the pits, and it was disgraceful that her daughter had to get a bus to the nearest town everyday just to make a living. My mother did her best attempt at making sympathetic noises over the garden wall, but she didn't like confrontation. It was a world she couldn't fully understand as the daughter of a professor, who'd been able to take her piano and clarinet lessons well and truly for granted. I watched as she made a beeline for the house with the washing basket when she heard the oven timer make imaginary noises.

My father couldn't pronounce the house name at first. He'd roll his tongue around in his mouth to try and piece the syllables together, choking on the double-l in Wenallt, and, eventually, on the saliva he'd produced as a result of his lingual exercises. It didn't really matter what he could or couldn't pronounce anyway, he never usually said much to any of us. That's why I couldn't understand Mum, always having a go at him for staring at the bulky computer monitor on the desk, and ignoring her when she went into his study with a mug of Yorkshire Tea and a packet of Seabrooks crisps. Although I hadn't been a particularly academic child, unable to recite my times tables or get my head around the solar system, I did have common sense. I found that it was easier to avoid Dad altogether. To stay outside in the holidays or go to my bedroom and line up my naked Barbie dolls, once the leaves in the garden had died and dropped from the skeletons of the trees, gone to sleep for winter.

We'd completed the move during the school holidays, and spent entire days running down the grassy lumps of land at the front of the house, colliding with the Christmas trees at the bottom where the earth was flat and damp. We'd only ever owned a small patch of grass and a few flowerbeds to call a garden, nothing like the towering giants that had the potential to become a tree *house* one day. But at night, those trees were silent and still. Needles from the conifer branches that would get lost in our hair and scratch our arms as we wrestled our way to the top, cast shadows into my room that clawed up the magnolia walls. I'd pull the duvet over my head so I could block them out with flowery bedding. When we first went to view Wenallt, an old man that was passing the garden told us that the wall in front of the trees had been built during a war. When I couldn't sleep, I imagined low-flying planes throwing cartoon bombs at the wall, desperate to take it down, but each brick remained in its place, sandwiched by thick cement. My duvet also helped to block out the sound of my parents 'debating' downstairs, which I'd worked out years before then was adult code for having a blazing row. I was probably the only child that wished my parents would get a divorce. Or better still, that Mum would move into one house and take her potted plants, and Dad would do the same, taking his whisky bottles and Jazz CDs to a different house or maybe even a flat. I knew how to cook

84

using an oven and the hob, and we could have each parent over on alternating weekends. That seemed to be a fairer deal than the one we had back then.

It was on the other side of our wall that we first met the farmer. We'd already heard him in the mornings calling for his black pig, Lucy, who would follow the echoes of his voice, and we'd watch her go to where the farmer was standing from the windows at the top of the house. He stood in front of us that day, but he was holding a lead attached to something that was far too small to be the pig. The farmer lifted my brother and I over the wall, and asked us our names. We'd only ever seen a fox in animated films or as stuffed toys on shop shelves, which we were never allowed to take home with us. He let us run our grubby hands down the back of his red coat, smoothing the under-fur with gentle, downwards strokes.

'You kids ever been in a digger before, 'en?' Jack and I shook our heads in response, and followed the farmer over the road to what was known as The Dump; even though it wasn't a place you could take your recycling bags and old batteries to. It was just ugly wasteland leading into a jungle of thorns and terracotta bricks that had been thrown at the unstable landscape, with intentions of hitting stray cats to hear their struggle to escape.

There was a sign at the end of our road informing the locals and lorry drivers that there was *no access to the colliery through Dynant Fach Road*. The coal washery was next to The Dump, so the limited access meant that nobody ever came down there to tell us off for playing where we shouldn't be. We'd sieve undisturbed through the treasure that you could only get to by skidding down a dirt track, made years before we'd got there by some of the older kids on the road, and then venture further out once we'd collected our loot in an old Tesco bag. The original trail makers had grown up by the time we'd started exploring, and lived in pebbledashed houses of their own in the next village. They didn't want fragments of pottery or broken water pistols cluttering up their downstairs cupboards. It was all for us.

I'd sometimes take the lumps of coal back and give them to dad if he was in an approachable mood, which he'd put next to our fireplace in the coal bucket he'd picked up at a car boot sale one summer. Dad would empty the bucket into the grate on special occasions, usually Christmas, before lighting the kindling placed underneath a mountain of black coal. The best piece I ever found down The Dump was still hot in my hands from baking in the sun, with a chunk of silver wedged into the side of it that I'd tried unsuccessfully to pick out to keep for myself. Dad kept that piece on his office desk and used it as a paperweight for when he did his marking. Once, I thought about asking him if I could keep it, or if we could perhaps share it. I geared myself up all morning and mentally prepared my speech, but as the day went on, the air became thick and the sky darkened with rolling clouds. The weather was always reflected in dad's mood. The adults said it was because he suffered with S.A.D, just like granddad, but even with that explanation, I couldn't work out how somebody could catch a feeling and never seem to get rid of it. I sometimes worried that if granddad and dad had both caught it, perhaps I would too. I put off asking for my coal until another day, admiring it instead on my rare trips to the study.

Soon after we'd all reached The Dump, the farmer lifted us up again, but that time, it was me he lifted first. His fingers dug into my armpits, and I felt conscious of my ten-year-old body as my T-shirt came up to expose the butterfly tattoo above my belly button, that Mum had helped put on that morning with a damp flannel. He put my brother in the seat of the digger next to mine, and Jack put his hands on the steering wheel, his palms too small to grip the leather properly. The farmer rested his head on the rolled down window and told me I could press some buttons if I liked. His breath was warm and smelt like vinegar. He told me they were going to try and make a park with swings on the wasteland when the weather got better, and he was there with his digger to start preparing the land. He told me he had a granddaughter around my age and that she came to visit sometimes on weekends. I sat in diffidence, tugging at the belt loops on my jeans as Jack made digging noises and pretended to scoop dirt up with the claw at the end of the crane.

The farmer's fox sat at the wheel on my brother's side and started barking with urgency, in high-pitched bursts. We all looked up, even Jack, who had by that point climbed over the hard seats into the back of the JCB. The farmer jerked his head away from the window on my side and took a step back. Mum was running down the drive towards us with something black in her right hand, while Dad followed at a slower pace, hands deep in his corduroy pockets where he kept his hankies. I slid down to where the pedals were, the biggest one pressed on my ribs.

'Em? Jack? Kids, look up! Look!'

Mum had the camera we'd take on beach holidays in her hands, making sure she was standing a safe distance from where the fox was sitting, before looking at us through the lens and clicking. As we were all walking back up the drive, she kept gushing about what an incredible experience we'd just had with the lovely farmer, and how lucky we were to have been in a real digger. She didn't tell us off for leaving the garden with a man we didn't know like I'd expected her to. In this new country, everything seemed to be backwards from what we'd learnt, like in the *Magic Faraway Tree* in the Land of Topsy Turvy.

Samuel Hulett

Flood Pain

I rolled out of bed, trudged downstairs and sloshed through the water to the kitchen, where I began making Lara's breakfast.

Lara came into the kitchen with a splash. She grinned and hauled herself onto her chair at the table. She was small for her age and watched everything with great interest. She had seen me make breakfast before, obviously, but her mousy head swung around the room to keep track of the toast and tea. She chattered incessantly, about school — her whole life — and the news. Brexit was a favourite, a catastrophe I struggled to explain to her. Eventually I got her fed, made sure her insulin was sorted, and got her on the bus to school.

The spaces by the pharmacy were full, so I parked further away and walked, my feet soaked by the ankle-high water by the time I arrived. There had been a spate of migraines at work because of the late autumn sun glinting off the water's surface.

The pharmacist had gone to school with me. I saw him daily, but knew very little about him. He used to live in the street over from mine. One of life's strange little quirks that we should both find ourselves in the same city, miles from where we grew up.

'How's Lara today?' he asked as he gave me her prescription.

'Chipper as always, went off to school without a backwards glance. She's always reading. I don't get it.'

'I always hated school,' he laughed. I could have carried on, but the lady behind me in a beige overcoat was tapping her foot. I said my good byes and left for work.

A few weeks later the water was up to the top of the bottom stair and much colder. I set about making breakfast, as usual. Hearing the symphony afoot, the thunder of the kettle and the sawing of the bread, Lara joined me.

I had the radio on, listening to the news, though there was the danger it would invite a thousand questions from Lara. Instead, she listened intently to the straight-laced voice.

'The Intergovernmental Panel on Water Levels published its review today. Governments must commit to keeping global rising to 1.5 metres, by 2030, or risk catastrophic, irreversible — '. Lara protested as I switched to something less depressing and found more updates on Brexit, which drowned out everything else, like white noise.

'I was listening to that,' Lara complained.

'It's too early for that, Lara, we'll look at the news tonight instead.' There was a little more protest, but eventually a bargain was struck; her insulin administered, off to school she went.

There was a longer queue than usual in the pharmacist, and Eric looked harangued, red faced and sweating.

'Sorry for the wait. We're short on a lot of stock today. There's been issues with supply chains. We don't have Lara's insulin in yet. I'll have it in tomorrow; can you get it then?'

'Sure, I've got enough for a few days. You'll definitely have it in tomorrow?'

'Promise.'

'Okay,' I said, as sympathetic as I could. 'Keep on keeping

on.' He gave a little half smile and turned to the next customer, who charged the desk, furious.

Outside the chemist, the October air was warm as summer and the sun was bright and fierce, low, like it was setting. It set all the water in the streets alight, paving them with liquid fire. I stood a moment and appreciated the strange phenomenon, the warm air and the low sun, creating summer and sunset on an October morning. My shins began to get cold and I had to move on.

Lara was up before me. I sloshed through the knee-high water to where she was perched and ruffled her hair, eliciting a groan.

'Hello, early bird, caught any worms yet?' This prompted another sleepy groan. 'What woke you up, dear heart?'

'The police, Dad. They found a man who was ill on the street. The lights kept coming in my curtains. I opened my window and overheard them.' Fear fluttered in my stomach. What happened?

After breakfast was made and Lara was chewing enthusiastically on a jam-smeared crust, I went into the watery street to see what had been going on.

Down the street, my elderly neighbour was returning home, in floral wellies and lavender dressing gown. Her lined face amplified her scowl.

'Morning. Did they wake you too? Bloody blue flashing bastards.'

'Not me. Lara. What's going on?'

'Poor homeless feller died. Someone found him early this morning. Exposure.' She stood in her doorway and peered at the sky like it was hiding something. 'Never used to be like this,' she said, cryptically. 'You look after that girl. If you need anything, you come 'round, alright?'

I assured Hannah we would, and went to check on Lara. She was no worse for wear after lost sleep. Insulin checked, I put her on the school bus, which cruised off down the street with a wake, and went to my car.

It was out of petrol. I'd forgotten. I'd gone to the petrol station last night, and they were out. Had been for weeks. Disrupted supply lines, they said. I got half way down the street before the car finally gave a cough and died. I pushed it into a parking space and forgot about it.

I optimistically dug out a red plastic canister and sloshed to the petrol station. When I arrived, my hips were crying with the exhaustion of wading through knee-high water.

They were still out. An unhappy man at the till explained there was no sign of supplies getting through, and that trade in ready meals and sweets wasn't really enough to keep him in business.

At a loss, I abandoned my car and my crap plastic cannister and walked to the pharmacy. There, Eric — poor red, blood pressure bursting Eric — told me they were out of insulin, too. He had deep purple rings around his eyes and every time the door to the pharmacy shut, he shrank from the sound.

'Are you alright?'

'My wife can't get her pain medication,' he said, close to tears. 'She doesn't sleep.' I didn't know what else to say, so I patted him ineffectually on the arm.

'I'm so sorry, Eric. Let me know if there's something I can do.' He smiled thinly.

'Thank you. You'll have to go to the dispensary at the hospital, I don't know the next time we'll have any in.'

The hospital was miles away. I phoned work and explained. They weren't happy about it, but I didn't care. I waded to the hospital.

We only had enough bread for Lara's breakfast. It was weeks since we'd had tea. On the windup radio, someone was talking Brexit, again.

I struggled through the thigh-high water to the radio and angrily flicked it off. Brexit. What a goddamned vanity project. Every day things were getting worse, with no bread on the shelves, for God knew what reason, and yet we were being treated to this porcine waffling twenty-four hours a day.

I took Lara to school, towing her in a small rubber dinghy; she was too small to walk through the water any more. Once she was safely in school, I trekked to the hospital.

There was a different man at the dispensary. He looked a lot less harassed than the last man, a small, pale fellow. This man was much larger and two wet policemen in funeral-black uniforms stood on either side of the room, making very few ripples in the water, very, very conspicuously still. Someone must have tried to rob the pharmacy. I had got Lara's insulin from the other guy for the last few weeks, but I couldn't tell you what his name was. I hoped he hadn't been hurt in the robbery. Perhaps he was upstairs, on a gurney.

'I'm sorry, I can't give you any today. You'll have to come back tomorrow,' the new man said. For the last few weeks the quantity they gave out dropped, and now Lara was down to a few days' worth at most.

'I have to have some today.' I gripped the counter in frustration, the unfamiliar, barely contained fury which coiled quickly in my throat, ready to pounce.

'I'm sorry, we don't have enough to give you. We know you received enough last week. Come back tomorrow and you'll be on a priority list.'

'What happens when you run out, but I'm still at the top of the priority list?' I snarled.

'That won't happen, sir.' The man smiled, insincerely. I slammed my hand down on the counter. There was a ripple as one of the policemen behind me turned, but before they took offence, I stormed out, the dramatic effect numbed by the torpid sloshing of the water.

*

Hannah, Mrs Wilks, pressed the key to her house into my hand four or five days ago, before being borne off by one of the orange RIBs doing service as ambulances. 'Look after her,' she'd said, looking at Lara, who clung to the doorway of our house. The water was up to Lara's armpits now, my waist. I hadn't seen Mrs Wilks since.

There was plenty for breakfast. The bread was slightly stale, and I should have rationed the beans, but Lara had been so unwell lately, I wanted to cheer her up. I didn't tell her where I go it. Mrs Wilks must have been stock-piling. I went in through the back door like a sneak, and while Lara enjoyed hers, mine tasted of guilt. Guilt tasted like burnt toast and beans.

I got Lara into her dinghy and walked to the hospital. On the way, as we pushed past cars that were starting to float, I wondered whether I could get my hands on a RIB or a row boat or something so I didn't have to wade through waist-high water.

I prayed, on the way to the hospital. I hadn't prayed for years. I never normally did. I gave it a go when Lara's mother was ill, and when that didn't work, I stopped. I took it up again, hoping, fearing.

They were out, of course. It had been weeks since we had

been able to get any, and I was already giving Lara half doses. I didn't know what to do. I tried to hide it from her. I stood in the street outside the hospital, clutching the white rope on the edge of her dinghy, unsure where to go or what to do next.

I stood there in the low sun, Lara watching a lichen-spotted stick bobbing in the road. It had fallen from a dying, water-logged tree. The tree was rotting where it stood, roots submerged, its bark blackened and slimy by the sloshing street. Behind it the pilings of an old house gate were rusting and its masonry crumbling as its mortar dissolved. Where had all the water come from? How long had it been there? Wasn't anyone doing anything about it?

I was trying to remember when I last heard birdsong, when the roar began. It began around the corner, bouncing strangely from the house fronts. For a second I thought it was another RIB, before I realised it was the roar of a wave.

I dragged Lara's dinghy away from the sound as swiftly as I could. Weak and cold, I was slow in the waist-high water. I could hear it behind us, eating the street swiftly with its white teeth. Bang followed bang as it bounced already floating cars aside.

It was on us, too fast, and I lost my footing in the rushing water. I struggled to stand, then breathe, as the cold, dark water shoved me down. My arm jerked as the wave took the dinghy. I heard Lara scream 'Dad!' above the watery throb and hiss. I clung with all my strength to the rope, which sawed against my closed fist. My skinny arms and legs were no match for the heavy water, gripping and pressing me like dead hands, pulling at my limbs, prying at my mouth. My hand clenched tighter around the white nylon rope.

The water calmed and in the slack I found my feet, breaching in the bright early morning light. I gasped and retched, and saw the red and yellow dinghy.

It was empty. Lara was missing

I splashed around the gently bobbing cars, screaming for her, but she was nowhere to be found. My heart beat a vital tattoo, but felt numb like my feet and the cold wet tips of my fingers.

I called for help, up to my midriff, bellowing in the watery street.

I couldn't find her anywhere. Lara was gone.

Theo Elwyn Hung

Painted Sky

Who painted the sky?

Was it the human?

Sending their dreams up under the radiant moon, creating
stars.

To think when I look up so too did my father and his father
before him.

Ancestors in line, all staring at the same sky.

Or.

Was it mother nature?

The original architect.

She who protects,

She who nurtures this world.

She who dug her hands into the sands of the Sahara and
scattered it in to the sky;

Creating stars.

Or.

Was it divine?

Unimaginable. Unfathomable. Incomprehensible power.

The same divine that snapped its fingers and it all came to
be.

I believe it was divine.

For only the divine can create such delicate beauty

Katya Johnson

Folly Farm

Sorcia settled down on the only space on the long, sawdust-strewn bench that she could find in the shade. The day was unbearably hot – a scorching Saturday spent on the outskirts of Swansea, in a June that broadcasters had described as the hottest on record. Now, dressed in her all-black outfit and chunky boots, Sorcia felt distinctly uncomfortable. She had walked ahead of the rest of the party to find a seat before the show began. They had last been seen at the meercat enclosure, where Jonathan had whipped the small rodents into a state of manic excitement by feeding them handfuls of wilted green lettuce and carrot shavings that he had clandestinely bought in for the purpose. Her mother and stepdad had turned a blind eye: 'What they won't know can't harm them,' professed Sheena, referring to the zoo staff. 'Anyway, it's what I love about small zoos – they let you get so close to the animals.'

A man with arms roiling in inky tattoos emerged from the door of a small wooden hut, carrying two large plastic boxes. He released them gently onto a wooden plinth erected in front of the spectators' benches. Sorcia regarded them sceptically: they were precisely the same domestic storage boxes that her parents used to retain Jonathan's ever-growing Lego collection at home. 'Mum, Dad, Jonathan, they're about to start,' she trumpeted loudly, though she knew her announcement was futile. As it was Jonathan's big day, her parents were even more likely to indulge him than usual. In reality, they could be any length of time.

By now a small crowd had gathered to watch the reptile show in the small, provincial zoo. Sorcia observed them passively: a corpulent family speaking in soft Liverpudlian accents congregated on the right-hand-side of the spectators' ring; a bored-looking girl with a T-shirt bearing the slogan 'Eat Prey Love' tapped away at a phone a few metres away, and on another row of benches a flustered blonde mother reined in a toddler on an elasticised waistband. She raised an immaculately-plucked eyebrow at Sorcia, who was sitting moodily and defiantly on her own.

Sorcia had always detested the concept of zoos. She had converted to vegetarianism at the age of thirteen, when she had encountered a grisly platter of pigs-in-blankets at a family Christmas party. Ever since that day she had denounced marbled rashers of bacon, roast dinners and every other form of animal exploitation and cruelty, as a barbaric crime. For this reason, both Sheena and Mark were amazed when Sorcia agreed to join them on their outing to Folly Farm for Jonathan's tenth birthday. Privately, she had only relented when her friends in Sixth Form told her that Folly Farm rehomed rescue animals.

Sorcia heard a loud, wheezing cough from the stage. 'Ladies and gentlemen, boys and girls, welcome to the reptile show! Croeso!' The zookeeper smiled in a grisly, toothless fashion at his audience and the petrol sheen of his sunglasses glinted in the sunlight. Sorcia scanned around her, but her family were still nowhere to be seen. 'For those of you who've not met me before, my name's Gareth and I'm the Head Zookeeper and Superintendent of Animals here at Folly Farm. Today, as it's so warm, I'm going to bypass the lizards and, instead, focus on three remarkable snakes we look after here.'

Sorcia looked up at the zookeeper again. She noticed how tough and leathery his skin was, as if coated in a primordial layer of mud, and the dilapidated condition of the clothes he wore – his khaki trousers were patched and faded, and his battered outdoor boots were held together by mismatching shoelaces.

'Alright then, let's get started. The first slippery fella I want to introduce you to is called Bernie. And as you can see…' the zookeeper clicked open the first box on his right and plunged his hands in, 'Bernie has very vibrant colouration.'

The audience released a collective 'Ahh.' Even Sorcia had to admit that the snake was beautiful: striped in longitudinal bands of scarlet, obsidian black and cream rings. 'Commonly confused with the deadly coral snake, this species of snake is called a kingsnake and is a non-venomous constrictor.'

Sorica watched as the zookeeper stroked the seething flank of the red snake, which coiled itself in tight, neat loops about his arms and hands. Its forked tongue momentarily darted out of an invisible mouth.

'Kingsnakes have earned their name for a reason. Though they're not the biggest snakes, they are immune to the venom of other snakes and even eat them. Despite this, I would always recommend the Californian kingsnake as a first snake. Though they can be a bit nippy if they're not handled enough, they are outgoing, lively companions and very easy to look after. Snakes are predators and it is natural that they bite from time to time – it shows their predatory instincts are still intact.'

The zookeeper smiled amenably at his audience, but they didn't seem particularly persuaded by his logic. The little girl sitting to Sorcia's right had relinquished her phone, and instead sat rigidly staring at the prehensile serpent oozing about the keeper's arms. The mother gathered her toddler into her arms and installed it into a nearby pram. It was then that Sorcia spotted her family. They were walking quickly in the direction of the reptile show, with Jonathan in the vanguard. Her mother waved enthusiastically at her from a distance. Sorcia shuddered with embarrassment. The zookeeper hadn't yet noticed the new arrivals as he was busy extricating specimen number two from its plastic tub.

'This here, folks, is Wimpy, more commonly referred to as a ball python or a royal python...' Gareth brandished the reptile before his audience with paternalistic pride.

Sorcia could see why; this snake was utterly different from the last one, but just as distinctive; with creamy, leopardlike markings outlined in black, set against luscious, caramel-brown scales. Her mother and stepdad sidled in next to her.

'Hi honey, we lost you,' her mother cooed warmly, from under her broad sunhat. She grasped her shoulder tightly but Sorcia shrank away from her and the repellent, sticky smell of sun lotion she emanated. She couldn't help notice that Jonathan wasn't with them. Instead he had elected to sit on a thick band of rope looped between poles positioned daringly close to the perimeter of the exhibiting table. A little knot began to form in Sorcia's stomach. Gareth looked at the boy quizzically but didn't stop mid-sentence.

'Like the kingsnake, ball pythons are constrictor snakes, which means that they kill their prey through asphyxiation. Occasionally, when they get frightened, they curl up into a ball – hence the name. They are indigenous to Africa and there is a certain tribe in Nigeria that consider this snake sacred...'

'The Igbo Tribe.'

The voice was young, high-pitched and steeped in

patronising superiority – it could only belong to one person. Sorcia's skin tingled with irritation. Gareth turned to the young boy sitting nonchalantly by his side.

'Is that right? Well thank you very much for that clarification.' Just before he was about to resume, he turned back again and scrutinised the boy for a few seconds longer. 'I think I've seen you here before.'

'Yes, Jonathan loves Folly Farm – this is his fifth visit,' piped up Sheena brightly from among the general audience. 'We've come here on a special trip today, for his tenth birthday.'

'Well, happy birthday Jonathan,' the zookeeper grimaced. His hands seemed to tighten on the writhing snake. Two fluffy black flies buzzed onto Sorcia's naked calf, then buzzed off again.

'Happy birthday!' echoed the members of the audience. Sheena was beaming, Sorcia's stepdad, Mark, grunted and Jonathan smiled in a way that artfully concealed his gappy teeth.

'Ok folks, well here's a cool fact about the royal python. In Africa, these snakes are considered so beautiful and placid that they're worn by tribe rulers as jewellery. So let's have a go – try Wimpy on for size. He's a super friendly snake and very docile, so don't be shy.'

Gareth brought Wimpy over to the family groups one by one. A number of children stroked him, following sly encouragement from their parents. Even Sorcia allowed Gareth to place Wimpy in her lap. She stroked him gingerly with the tips of her fingers, noting how cool the milky white underbelly of the snake was despite the heat wave. Sensing an opportunity to share a moment with her daughter, Sheena also placed her hand on the snake's body, now wedged against Sorcia's thigh. Sorcia thought of the plethora of genuine fur coats and leather handbags hanging in her mother's wardrobe at home and felt instantly sick.

Jonathan was the last person to handle the snake. He took him into his hands and grinned as the snake twisted about his arms and shoulders. 'It tickles!' he shrieked once with glee, but still refused to return the snake to the animal keeper. At last Jonathan conceded and two anonymous helpers whisked the plastic boxes back inside the wooden hut.

'Alright. Now strap on your seatbelts and hold tight. This is the moment we've all been waiting for. This next snake is a guaranteed first. It is, as of this year, one of the largest snakes kept in any institution in Wales and by far the oldest and longest of the snakes we've got here at Folly Farm. For this reason, it will require three members of staff to lift it today. This might take a few minutes...'

Gareth dissolved into the darkness of the hut with his two minions and the crowd hummed in anticipation. The animal keepers returned some moments later, staggering beneath the shared weight of the mighty animal. Jonathan was so entranced by the sight of the serpent that he got in their way and tripped up Gareth, who was carrying the bulk of the weight in his arms.

Come on Jonathan, sit over here now, with us,' expostulated Mark, but Jonathan ignored him and obstinately resumed his seat on the rope.

'Right, well we got there in the end,' observed Gareth, throwing his audience a brave, battle-weary smile, once the snake had been safely deposited on the table. 'Thanks to Jess and Rachel my brave assistants.' There was a tokenistic round of applause. 'And now welcome Mango on stage!'

Now the applause was genuine. The sight was so remarkable that even Sorcia stood up for a better view. The vast black snake was coiled up on the table like an impossibly distended stretch of ribbon. Its girth was as thick as three human necks; its flesh muscled, coiled and tensed. Its unguent, black skin glinted maraudingly in the sun.

'Mango is a female Burmese python – one of the five largest species of snake in the world. At twenty years of age, she weighs just over a hundred-and-ten pounds. Mango's favourite food is bunny rabbit. So you can see why we don't do public snake feedings…' This quip raised a polite laugh from the adults. 'Obviously, in the wild, we would all be an attractive option for this snake who runs five times faster than…'

'Snakes don't run,' interrupted Jonathan petulantly. 'They slither.'

The zookeeper glared at the little boy beside him for a few seconds and muttered something below his breath, but resolved, heroically, to keep going. 'Okay, they slither… you know what I mean. O Duw!' Gareth suddenly exclaimed, 'You made me break my chain again.'

For a second Sorcia wondered what Gareth meant by this, but then she realised it was shorthand for chain of thought. The zookeeper obviously wasn't a natural public speaker and Jonathan wasn't making it any easier for him.

'Right, well I can't remember what else I was going to say, so let's move on. Now, obviously, Mango is too big for me to bring her to you. So instead I'd ask that you come up here to the table to handle her if you want to…'

Jonathan was the first one to jump up and approach the grossly oversized snake on the table, but he was soon joined by others. Sheena went up with Mark and every member of the family from Liverpool waddled up to the table. Only the little blonde girl remained behind. Sorcia regarded her brother with a growing sense of exasperation. Today, his boastful attitude was getting even more on her nerves than usual, so she decided to stay put. If she got any closer, she knew she would end up saying something hurtful to him and didn't want to.

Suddenly a general cry was heard from the table. 'Stop!' It was Sheena. 'Jonathan, stop it.'

A general roar went up. 'You stupid twerp,' shouted the zookeeper, unable to control himself. The reason soon became clear: Jonathan had grabbed hold of the snake's tail, and was waggling it around in the air like a pair of maracas.

'Snakey, snake! Shakey, shake!'

'For God's Sake,' screamed Sheena, 'Jonathan, put it down.'

By this point, Sheena's face has crimsoned to a deep shade of beetroot red, but it was too late. In a matter of seconds, the giant snake propelled itself in one graceful parabolic arc onto the young boy's body, crushing him to the ground.

'Somebody help him now!'

'Fool,' Sorcia almost wanted to scream. 'Serves him right.' Her head was ringing, but two bodies launched themselves into the fray simultaneously – her mother's and Mark's.

The little boy whined and moaned as the snake tightened its grip around his arms and chest. Gareth shoved away the parents and began to wrestle with the enormous reptile like a superhero of the ancient world. At an opportune moment, he reached down into one of his bulging pockets and impaled the underside of the snake's throat with a tranquiliser dart. The vast black serpent went slack, pinning Jonathan down under one hundred kilos of prime, slack black flesh.

The scene was one of utter confusion. Jonathan had lost consciousness and when Gareth at last managed to extricate him from underneath the snake, he laid him out on the exhibiting table like an etherised patient in an operating theatre.

Sorcia was filled with a sudden, irrepressible urge to act. As the other animal keepers had run for help, she knew she had only a matter of minutes. So, shielded by the furore, Sorcia slipped unobserved into the dark black entrance of the hut where she saw two white boxes by the door. With a confident and well-practised hand, she clicked back the lids and slid them off. Casting a sorrowful glance back at the magnificent python lying unravelled and senseless on the ground, Sorcia stoically resumed her seat beside the young blonde girl. Without speaking, they both watched the end of the reptile show – as two snakes, one with leopard-like markings, and the other the colour of rubies, slithered unnoticed between the parched rocks of Folly Farm and out into the open countryside.

Jaffrin Khan

Skin

Colonisation sits in my bones;
as I'm sitting at home and they tell me,
Unfold your legs and sit with respect,
Because being brown was all about what people thought of
    me and what people saw in
me
'Our women don't fold over their legs' they said
See, nor do the women in the Royal family,
Is that what happened when we adopted their ideology?
Porcelain skin born into power,
Producing prejudice,
Power brings popularity,
And popularity bought my people.
When my friend is asked about the lightness in her skin,
She tells them that she's mixed with rape,
That the answer was rape,
That her grandmother was a child of rape,
That her great grandmother produced a child from being
    raped
By her slave master.
Colonisation swims in her blood.
My skin became many things but my own;
I was asked about the brown of skin and why it didn't
    blend in

Into the pinks of my palm
I wondered why God didn't blend my borders
Why was I an unfinished piece
and then
My body became many things but my own
It was as if I was Braille and the only thing he saw was
opportunity
blind to everything but desire
He needed to explore me
But he didn't asked me
And when I told him
He didn't belong here
He claimed he found a home in me
After discovering places in me I hadn't yet found for myself
He left my insides infested
And colonies in my memories
My skin would become terrorised by the Western standards
of beauty telling me what I
need to be
They had me scrubbing a little harder on my face to abolish
my pigmentation
They had me looking a little longer at the lightening
products on the shop shelves
They had me waking up earlier to straighten the culture
straight out of my hair
Glowing up they'd say
'Don't stay out in the sun,
You'll get too dark.'
And so I stay out in the sun,
Till my diamonds form on my face,
Till my complexion glistens gold,
Till my skin bakes my ancestors back to life to have their
stories retold.

Catrin Lawrence

A Modest Proposal

The cupboard's getting too small. It's like one of those priest holes Mum's been teaching me about when we do history. Catholics had to hide their priests when the Protestants wanted to burn them at the stake. Mum calls me her little priest. I've got to hide like them, which is stupid cause I'm not Catholic. I've never seen a cross at home, in here or the bit of hallway that leads to the bathroom. When I go there, Mum closes all the curtains and I run as fast as I can.

The cupboard used to be a toilet, but Mum took it out. Still smells. All my stuff's on shelves above my head. Loo-ming, which is a word I like cause it sounds scary. My camp bed squashes a bit at the end which used to be fine but now my feet push against it every night. Mum says it's cause I'm growing into a big strong lad like my brother David. He's the best. He comes in to read with me or to chat. We can't play video games in case we make too much noise.

"You're better off reading anyway," Mum says. "I'm not having you left behind cause of me."

Mum couldn't have me. It sounds weird, but when you get money from the gov-ern-ment (a spelling Mum wants me to learn), you can't have more than two kids. That's the rules.

But Mum says some rules are made to be broken. So I stay in the cupboard and get lessons from her. Mum's great at teaching, so great she wanted to be a proper teacher, but she never got the qualifications (I can spell that one backwards) cause she had Sarah. I'll get them though, one day, and we'll never need money from the gov-ern-ment again.

"Then you can have lots of babies." Mum laughs when I tell her. "Get a good job and have as many as you want."

"No. Babies are icky."

*

Sarah's getting married and Mum says I can share David's room. And go to proper school. Only thing is I have to say I'm her nephew and my parents died so she's looking after me now.

I get ready for the wedding before everyone, so I practise looking sad in the living room. If anyone asks me about my parents, I'll look convincing. There's lots of photos of Mum, Sarah and David. Girly giggles from Mum's room. David trying to sing along to his rock music, as loud as he wants now. I taste the perfume and Lynx from here. Spit in my hands.

Looking sad's getting boring and it's hard when everyone's so happy. I'll see what Outside looks like. Three grey blocks coming out of the ground, with balconies. The little glass towers far away are cooler, like spaceships. I'll work in one of those when I'm older.

Some policemen walk past the window. Without the curtains closed.

Into the cupboard. I make myself small in a corner. They'll burn me like the Catholics. Bang. Yelling through the walls. I'll be smaller.

"What's going on?"

"Where's Sam?"

"If they come in here, I'll kill them."

Running past the cupboard. Mum says a bad word in the living room. She runs back.

"Sam? Sam!"

"I'm here."

She crawls in the cupboard and hugs me tight. She puts her hands over my ears, but the yelling still goes on like I'm underwater. There's something wet in my hair.

"They're not here for you, baby, they're not here for you," Mum mumbles.

There's a ghost above us. I scream but the light turns on and it's Sarah in her wedding dress. "Mum, it's okay. They're gone."

"I thought…" Mum says.

"David's watching to make sure, but I think it's just next door. Dragged the kids off."

"All of them?" She nods. "In demand, aren't they?"

That means when you want something really badly. But if we can't have kids, who wants them?

*

"We have an honoured guest for our debate today," Mr Smith says. "Students, please welcome Bexleyheath and Crayford's Member of Parliament."

I straighten my tie and stand with the others. I still feel crooked, slouched. Don't know why; I passed Eleven Plus like everyone else. A boy from Hackney across the room (we catch the same Tube to school) tenses too, then sees me. We grin.

Everyone sits when the MP does. Dust specks drift between our teams in a slant of sun.

"Today's motion: 'The two-child benefit cap should be repealed.' Discuss."

The cap. We talk about it all the time, in citizenship class and in history. It's like my life's being chucked on the table for

110

discussion. If I get too upset about it, the teachers might ask questions. When Mr Smith put me on opposition I nodded. Keeping quiet keeps me safe.

Opposition starts, and we talk such shit. Not enough money to go around (bet some of them have), who needs more than two kids (the girl who said that is one of four). The worst one is when someone suggests the kids will be better off with different parents. Yeah right. I went into primary two years ahead of everyone cause of Mum.

Affirmative team isn't doing better. There's stuff about the economy growing and human rights, but nobody talks about kicked-down doors and screaming kids. Not meaning to exist. The Hackney boy says something about estate rumours, like the stuff Sarah believes. It's bad enough as is, never mind if the kids are being turned into glue.

It comes back to the opposition. To me. I stand. Mr Smith said the hardest part of debate is when you've got to argue for something you're against. I can't stay quiet. Sorry, Hackney.

"The rumours addressed by the speaker are spread to disincentivise people from breaking the law. It's an advantage of the system. The children aren't punished like their parents."

Mr Smith's head bobs up and down, to me then the MP. He mouths: Good student. One of my best.

The MP's sweat shines like he's cooking. He shakes his head and walks out.

*

"You've got to try this, lads." Andrew taps his fingers on the bar as the bottle clunks down. "Asian giant hornets brewed in vodka. It's an aphrodisiac, which, if you listened in biology like a good boy, means you can be a very bad boy later."

"Think you need a girlfriend to benefit from that," I say.

111

The lads shake on their barstools, hooting with laughter.

"Alright, calm down, Scholarship," Andrew says, but he grins.

Andrew's friend pushes away the dish of cricket gambas. Poor sod's the only vegetarian in The Roasted Snail. Everything's made from insects.

"Sam, you'll have a cricket, won't you?"

"Course." A spicy crunch between my teeth. "Not like there's anything else to eat."

"I mean…" the vegetarian says.

"I meant meat," I laugh. "Wait till I'm a solicitor. I'll get fat off the stuff."

"Not even then," Andrew says. "I haven't had meat since Christmas. Father could afford a whole herd, the cheap bastard."

A 'chef wanted' sign on the chalkboard. I text the details to Mum's boyfriend. It's a bit far, but the family might like it better in Oxford. A better life for his two kids and he can come off Jobseekers. So could Mum, with the salary he'd be getting here. No more kids in the cupboard.

"But you've had meat?" I say to Andrew.

"I forget sometimes you haven't," Andrew sighs, elbows on the bar. "Pork and beef and all sorts."

The lads get his look.

"Sausages wrapped in bacon."

"Sausages wrapped in bacon."

"Please tell me you've all had lamb."

"But you know what the best is."

"Should we really be talking about this?" The vegetarian looks at me. We're on our first pub and he's pale.

"I'm fine. They're not rubbing it in. Andrew, which did you say you liked?"

The vegetarian picks up a cricket. A crack between his forefinger and thumb. We, and the cricket, stare at him.

"If I ate this cricket right now, will you buy my drinks the rest of the night?"

Andrew grins and reaches into his pocket.

"Only if I can film it."

*

Cicadas for starters. A glazed pile, ringed by cucumber and lemon slices. Like shit dressed up. It won't offend my boss if I refuse. But only having champagne makes me look like I'm here to get drunk. Everyone else from Highdale Solicitors has a glass in one hand, cicada in the other.

"It's the shells that get me," I say to my boss, waving away the tray.

"I understand. Insects can be irritable. The stuff we'll put in our mouths! But the main course…" He takes a slow sip. I do the same. "Will be red meat," he continues.

Saliva coats the inside of my mouth. "It's kind of you to get it in for us."

"I wanted to celebrate. It's been a good year, especially with the trainees. Some I'd bring onto the firm straightaway if I could."

He gives me a look. I'll eat every tray of cicadas if that means what it means.

His wife comes over and smiles at us. Her perfume hints at lilies but the smell from the dining room is the biggest hint at luxury.

"Looks like dinner's served. I'll see you in there."

I go to the toilet before dinner starts. Quick, so I don't return to bones. I'll phone Mum later. A job in sight. Red meat. Everything I've worked for starts here.

The downstairs toilet is bigger than my childhood cupboard. When I'm a solicitor, I'll get Mum a bigger place.

Now I'm alone I can turn my phone on. Caleb smiles back at me, blue eyes from Mum's boyfriend, matching the jumper I sent him. It's stupid of Mum but it doesn't matter now. That benefits cap will never hang over us again. That cupboard will stay empty.

Fifty missed calls from David.

"David?"

"Where the fuck you been?"

"Firm's policy. Work phones only during the day."

"What, you been sleeping there? I've been trying to call you since yesterday."

Yesterday I worked till midnight on a case.

"God, I'm sorry. I've been working on my training contract."

"Mum's killed herself."

I hold the phone from my ear. Tears spill over.

"Why? How? What about…"

"She jumped off the balcony. The police cuffed her, but she ran…"

"Police?"

"Someone tipped them off about Caleb."

God. I grip the sink. Champagne sways in my stomach.

"She said she knew what they'd do to her boy. She couldn't take it."

"I can do something. Challenge the council in court. It's too late for Mum." I rip off some toilet paper. Wipe my eyes. Down a sob. "But we can get the kids back."

"Sam. It's too late." Laughter from the dining room. "Where are you?"

"Boss's house. We're about to have dinner. I'll make an excuse and go."

Everyone's joking and chatting as I enter. I catch my boss's eye.

"I'm sorry, there's been a family emergency."

"I can see from your face. Take some food with you, you'll pass out."

"That's kind of you, but I'd rather be going as soon as... Stop."

His carving knives hover above the roast. Crouching on a silver platter. Crispy skin puckered from flesh. The smell. Sweet, like Mum say babies smell. She was right.

"Davidson? Was there something you wanted to say?"

Closer. Blue glass eyes. Caleb's shade. His smile gone, lips curled in like rinds.

"Davidson, you don't look well. Have some meat."

All my saliva, my anticipation, my meals from the days when I could've saved him on the floor. Tongue choking. Shaking.

"By God, is he drunk?"

"Well, if you're not used to champagne..."

I spit the last bits of vomit. It doesn't reach my boss's shoes.

"Davidson! Someone help him up, call him a taxi." He whispers, "Someone clean this mess."

Arms under my pits. Down the hall. Can I walk? Would I like water? They understand, they've seen the cook's face blanch whenever he orders red meat in. He gives the babies eyes to remind them back there what they're eating but they never care. Non-disclosure agreements but everybody knows.

"That's going to put me off my dinner."

"Now that's unfair. Andrew said he's from the East End. It might be his first time drinking champagne. He'll get used to it. Anyway. Leg or breast?"

James Lloyd

Moving House

The rooms are empty

a gallery
with the paintings
                    removed

They left
cut out
        shadows on the wall

phantoms of the furniture
          impress their footprints
in the past

Walking through
the disfamiliar space
urges me to leave my mark

to press a primitive palm
and blow a blood red negative
leaving nothing but
                        myself

Instead I'll write a poem
huddled in that new house

strange
        as another man's boot
we will slowly mould to fit.

Jonathan Macho

Weeds

It was the fourteenth day of the fifteenth month and he was still pulling up the weeds.

Pull. Pop. Almost every one came up the same. A little tug to work them out, a little pop as the root came free from the gravel. Big, small, intricate, maddeningly simple. It took so little effort that he wondered if the others judged him sometimes. If they thought that he had gotten off easy.

Pull. Pop.

The problem wasn't the effort though, was it? It wasn't the struggle, the sweat, the blood of the work. The problem was it never seemed to stop.

Pull. Pop.

Pull. Pop.

For every weed that he removed, there was a hundred more. For every hundred, a thousand just out of sight. The rock garden stretched the length of the temple, and he worked his way down it, metre by metre, day by day. He had reached the end more than once, only to turn and see the tiny green shoots, budding flowers and stretching leaves trailing along behind, tracing his path, drawing him back. He was scared to reach the end of the garden again now. He knew the weeds would be waiting.

Pull. Pop.

Pull. Pop.

Pull. Pop.

When his Master had first shown him to the rock garden, had plucked a plant stem and root from between the stones and instructed him to see that all the others would follow, he had been lost. Such an easy task could provide no lesson of value. All through the garden, his fellows worked arduously, planting, tending and wresting up far more impressive things. Their quarry roared as it came away from the soil. His popped.

Pull. Pop.

"Master please," he had said. "I am ready for whatever you deem necessary. Whatever it takes. Don't go easy on me now."

Pull. Pop.

"Nothing about balance is easy," the Master replied, inscrutable. "This garden is kept in balance in countless ways, big and small. All of them are necessary."

Pull. Pop.

He wanted to say that he did not appreciate condescension. He wanted to demand a challenge that was actually challenging. He wanted –

Pull.

To learn. So he had said nothing and got to work.

Pop.

It had been slow going at first. He was a firm believer that if you had a job, you should do it to the best of your ability. Not only that; he wanted to impress. He made sure to carefully examine every centimetre of the garden, literally leaving no stone unturned. He was surprised by how easily he had found a rhythm. It felt… Meditative. Maybe that was the idea. That satisfying sound as the air escaped and the weed was disposed of…

Pull. Pop.

It had taken many weeks and more plants than he cared

to think about, but his first circuit had quickly turned satisfaction to obsession. The myriad shoots that had blossomed behind his back outraged him. He stormed to the Master and demanded retribution.

"They are plants, you know," came the answer. "Growing is what they do."

"But, but all my work…"

"I fail to see how that is relevant. You pulled up the weeds. Now there are more."

"So why do it in the first place?"

"You did it because I told you to do so. From the sounds of it, much remains undone."

Doubly defeated, he returned to the garden, sunk to his knees, and continued.

Pull. Pop.

Pull. Pop.

Pull. Pop.

It had become more than that, of course. The Master had clearly intended this to be the lesson, that elusive thing that would teach him everything he wanted to know. As soon as all the weeds were out of the soil and the rock garden was unblemished by green, he would be sure, or be ready to learn, and it would all be worthwhile.

Pull. Pop.

He had started to visit the garden out of hours. He knew that was discouraged; the work of the temple was spiritual as well as physical, and such things should not be forced. Still, on some rest days he would find himself walking in the grounds and the green spots scattered among the white would catch his eye. The time he was already putting in clearly wasn't enough. Getting a small lead might just give him an edge. He'd wander over, bend low, take a stem between his fingers and…

Pull. Pop.

The root itself was an ugly thing, lumpen and pale. Some were fatter than others, some longer. On the slowest days he wondered what that meant, whether it was age or location or just chance that warped the little things. The roots of the flowers differed from the roots of the grass which differed from the roots of the clovers, but they were all weeds in the end. They all kept growing back.

Pull. Pop.

When he had started it was hot on the gravel, the summer sun beating down as he wound his way. Colder, wetter weather had grown around him in the time since and loosened some of the tighter soil, making life a little easier. Even then, he wondered if it helped the weeds grow faster behind him, keeping that damned balance the Master had spoken of. He worked faster, as if to outsmart them all.

Pull. Pop. Pull. Pop.

He wasn't fast enough. Not yet.

Pull. Pop. Pull pop.

But given time he knew.

Pull pop. Pull-pop. Pullpop.

They couldn't outrun him forever.

Pullpoppullpoppull –

SNAP.

He looked down at the split stem in his hand. Damn. It had resisted and he had pulled too hard, too sharp. A stupid mistake. The root was still in the earth, buried by stones, hidden. If he left it there, it would just start growing all over again. He'd be here, again, in another fifteen months, plucking the exact same plant from the exact same spot. He could not let that happen.

He scrabbled in the gravel, worming fingers through the stones, feeling for anything soft. He had worked his hands raw doing this in the early days, before he had learned the rhythm of the work, and then again, back when he had first realised that the work had followed him around. The ground was harder then, and the earth now dampened his hands before it cut them. He didn't care anymore. All that time, it couldn't have meant nothing. He couldn't just let it mean nothing…

There. Something… Different. Wiry and loose and fibrous. He pulled and it came up like a cord, trailing through the stones, stretching and winding back around him. This was more than just the root of the plant he had discarded. This kept going and going… How far did it go? How much did it connect to?

An idea blossomed in his mind and it was too much to bear. What if they were all one weed? What if every one of the little, negligible sprouts he had torn free up to now were just heads of a much greater monster?

He couldn't face it. Getting to his feet, he left his work early for the first time in what seemed like an age and went to sit in the shadows of the temple wall. He wasn't sure how long he had been there when the Master and another pupil walked past, speaking in hushed tones.

"…a shame to see the rock garden untended," the Master was saying, "but the boy has been so consumed lately I fear he will never learn the lesson." It was like a dagger in his already reeling head. "That is why it falls to you to work on our ivy problem."

The pupil nodded. "Whatever you require, Master."

"Remember to take care, won't you?" The Master turned to regard the building, still not seeing the figure hidden by its shade. "Balance, as ever, is key. Cut it back, but the temple is old now and the ivy is a part of it. Sometimes I fear that it is the only thing holding the place together."

"Of course," the pupil said. "I will show restraint."

The Master smiled. "I am sure. Now I must go to my engagement. I will be back first thing tomorrow. I look forward to being able to see through my window again on my return…"

They moved out of earshot not long after, leaving him alone. He looked up at the walls above him. The rock garden had grown so large in his eyes that the ivy had been completely blotted out. It drenched the roof and plunged down, a green waterfall frozen before it could reach the floor. Now there was a sizable enemy. A noticeable enemy. A weed he could actually see as he uprooted it.

The Master's words stayed with him. 'The boy' he'd said. 'A shame' he'd called it. Obviously he wasn't the only one disappointed by his lack of progress. Well here was a lesson he could finally learn. He'd show the Master he was ready. He'd show that he could win.

He followed the pupil to the outhouse where the temple kept its tools. He had barely been there before. His job required nothing but himself. Sometimes he thought the others did not trust him with equipment. Maybe they were right not to.

He made sure to hit the pupil's head just hard enough. He wanted to render them unconscious for the next few hours, nothing more, and certainly nothing less. He found the key to the outhouse in their pocket and locked them in, just to be sure. He hefted the spade over his shoulder, checking the metal tip for blood as he went, and walked to the point on the outer wall where the ivy was at its thickest. It was there he would draw up his plans for the war.

On closer inspection, the ivy was very different from the weeds he was used to. It had all the surface elements: it was green, had stems and leaves and flowers, and did not belong.

Whereas his weeds poked through the cracks of the rock garden however, the ivy snaked along the wall, hiding its tendrils behind bursts of greenery. He leant close and saw shrivelled brown paper fingers, clinging to the masonry, holding the branches in place. There, he thought. That's where I start.

He tried to slip his own fingers under the ivy, looking for purchase. Its grip was too strong. There was no space between wall and plant. No simple pull-pop this time.

For reasons he could not fully understand, he started to smile.

The spade then. The brown fingers crumpled and came apart as its metal tip carved up and through them, and he heaved on the handle, the hardest work he'd done in months, and he could feel the weight of the ivy as the branch snapped. He laughed, and something like dust came from the plant and got into his nose and mouth. He coughed and spluttered and spat, but wouldn't be put off that easily. He raised the spade again, gritted his teeth and hauled the rest of the creeper free. He picked it up and set it to the side, as he would have done with any weed. Already his progress seemed so much more impressive. Imagine how it would look when the whole lot came down.

He set to work and he kept on working. He wasn't sure when he started and he had no idea when he would be done. Before long, he was sweating and panting despite the cold, exhausted as all his contemporaries must have been. That wouldn't stop him though. Not the smell of it, the taste of the dust, the cries coming through the walls; not even the snaps and cracks of the ivy slowly being replaced with the creaks and crumbling of stone could stop him now. He was winning. He would learn his lesson soon enough.

Before anyone could have expected it, the sun was rising

and the Master had returned. The expected pride was absent. Instead, there was only horror.

The ivy had wormed its way too deep into the temple. There was no overhang it would not hang over, no pipe it had not curled inside, no gap it did not fill. It slipped through window snaps and the cracks under doors, and it carved its way between brickwork and from the outside to the in. Not even the rest of the garden was safe; the ivy choked the trees that lined the outer walls and cracked the ground nearby, running like his roots, pulling it all in as one. It had indeed been the only thing holding the place together and he had found it all out. For the first time his war was won but the cost was the rubble he had to clamber over as he made his way to the Master.

"I've done it," he said, eager, breathless. "You see? I'm ready. Teach me my lesson."

For a moment, for the first time, the Master seemed lost for words. Finally, he started to cry. "Oh my boy, you were never meant to have done it. You were meant to learn that it is never really done, that the work does not end… You were meant to move on."

He looked at the crumpled old man, sobbing in wreckage, and wondered what he ever thought he could learn here. Dropping the spade and the keys to the outhouse at the Master's feet, he set off to find new ways to win.

It was a few nights later when the coughs woke him.

Deep, racking things, they clawed up his gullet and forced him upright. He staggered from his bedside and made it to the mirror, finding some light with which to see. For even as the cough abated, the scratching, creeping feeling remained. He opened his mouth wide in a pantomime scream and saw it curling in the darkness.

A green creeper, small and leafed, tickled the back of his throat.

And what, there, stretching from his ear? What brown fingers reached out from his nostril? And why wasn't it clearer…? What was blotting out the light…?

He could see it staring back at him. A little leaf blossomed below his eye.

A reflex long ingrained made him reach for the ear, the longest stem, slowly, delicately, take it between his fingers and…

Pull –

And then the pain, so much, flooding his body, reaching all the way through him, grasping tight and not letting go. He screamed and it shook the ivy in his throat. He was terrified that he could feel it growing.

Then he knew. The weeds had taken root. They were all that was holding him up too.

Millie Meader

Interview with a Welshman

"These buildings were so full of life, and you could spot that brickwork through the polluted air," David said, as he pointed to what was the Lamp Room.

I looked up at him and saw a faint smile; what was he thinking? I wish I had asked. But he was in awe of everything, even though we were walking amongst rubble and above broken tiles. David saw differently. Through his eyes, he reimagined the red and yellow brickwork and the round glass window, facing its front. He saw the bustle of miners, old and young, marching in for their lamps to illuminate the darkness underground. David felt the nudge of young boys hurrying to the baths, to change into their work-drags, before they start at six o'clock. To me, it was just wind, brushing against my jacket. We walked inside a building with no roof, that used to be the Power House and sat down in the corner. I placed my phone, a notepad and a bottle of water on the table. I asked David if he was ready, and pressed *record*.

April 1962,

I woke up to the sound of my father and brother, bickering in the kitchen. They were debating on which filling would go in to today's sandwiches for our lunch break; it was between jam or cheese. It was always cheese. It's half-past four on a

Monday morning and today is my first shift at the Navigation Colliery. I left school as a young boy of sixteen and joined the National Coal Board, to be an apprentice electrician. I spent my first year at a local Mining College, until it was time to be allocated. My name was called, I was sent to the Navigation Colliery in Crumlin. Crumlin was a fair trek from me, but it was good enough. I had to walk down to the bottom end of Arthur Street and wait for the five o'clock bus. My stomach kept turning and turning, the narrow roads made it worse. It would take thirty minutes to reach Crumlin, and for me to catch my breath. The fumes were not just outside, as I inhaled the smoke and choked on the tar, sticking to the back of my throat. The men were trying to get in as many cigarettes as possible. I looked around the bus and saw other boys of my age, I recognised some. Glyn Lewis, Ray Thomas and Alf James. I arrived at the Navigation Colliery and headed straight to the baths, a fellow worker showed me where to go. I walked over the bridge, past the screens and across the pit top. I reached the baths and changed my clothes, clocked on in the Lamp Room and then headed to the Electricians' Shop. This was all done by six o'clock. I was shown my area and went straight into work, repairing what was damaged. I'm talking units, service panels and cables. This was my element. Albeit a bit frightening at first, my mind was at ease and off to work I go! Mr. Idris Rees, the electrical engineer, told me my hours and when we would get paid. It was on a Friday. We would receive them in a brown envelope.

March 1964,

I've learnt that being underground was never pleasant, it was a very dangerous place to be. You never think of it really, only until something bad happens and then it devours your mind.

I was on afternoons today, starting at two o'clock and finishing at ten. Unfortunately, there was a man killed underground, I don't know his name. He was a local man and older than me. His death brought me back to the day I was first taken underground, it was a couple of weeks after I started. Each of us would collect our lamps and prepare ourselves for the drop. The step gates shut, signal rang, and the cage lifted. Your heart would pound to the rhythm of the miners striking the coal face. It went at an amazing speed to reach the pit bottom, then you began the long trek to your station. It brought home the reality of what I'm doing. All us men, come together to work, but we don't think of the risks we take every day we're here. We enjoy what we do, but this death made me think a little. It wasn't just about his final moments before the accident happened, but how his loved ones are feeling. I can hear the cries of his wife and mother. I can see his father's head tilt to the soiled ground. Friends and workers remain silent around the site, remembering who we lost and how harsh our job can be. What if his wife was told the news by the deputy, holding a young 'un in her arms? You must admire the women, every day they anxiously wait for us to return home. Every day they dread to hear the words, "We're sorry."

July 1966,

I was on a morning shift today and finished at three o'clock, which was great, as it gave me the chance to meet up with a few friends for a pint. I decided to stick around Crumlin and take a later bus home. Whilst in The Railway, word got around about that new film being released, *Arabesque*. It starred Sophia Loren and Gregory Peck, a part of it was filmed here. It was some big helicopter scene over Crumlin Viaduct, that's what I've overheard. I wouldn't know for definite, I was working afternoons at the time they filmed. It's a shame that Crumlin Viaduct is now dismantled, thanks to the Beeching Axe. I remember being a young boy of eight years old going across it. I don't remember where I was going, but I could never forget facing the height of Crumlin Viaduct. We were so high up, that the people you saw walking beneath were like ants. I closed my eyes at first, I was terrified. But my Mam told me we were safe, even though you could hear the wind hitting our carriage and cradling you slightly. The view was unforgettable, I even remember seeing the Navigation Colliery and the men separating the masses of coal by size. The filming of *Arabesque* was a very big deal and got everybody talking. Ray Thomas, one of the boys I went with, told me that his younger brother waited by Kendon Hill for Sophia and her team. He hid in the nearby woodland, not to be caught, just to see her limo. It drove people insane. Before heading to the Electricians' Shop, I remember seeing the frenzy of locals, watching on a nearby banking. For mothers, it was an ideal day out for their children, plus a chance for them to see Gregory. Based on the chatter, a lot of people have already gone to see the film. I don't see myself going anytime soon, but one day I might watch it.

August 1967,

It's officially one month until the closure of the Navigation Colliery, and I am absolutely gutted. I thought it was a rumour at first, but when a nearby colliery closed, I knew ours was next. This was my second colliery, since I went to one during Mining College, but the time I've had here is irreplaceable. Whilst at my first colliery, you had to stay concrete to floor in the Electricians' Shop, conducting that circuit. The moment I came here, you're suddenly free to go anywhere and learn everything. You were never bored at the Navi, you could spend a few weeks in each area and pick up a new skill for life. I remember the first time I stepped foot in the Winder House, it was immaculate with its polished brass. Somebody must've polished that panel every day. It wasn't just what you see and do that made the Navi a great place to work, but the people too. We were all there to do the same thing and that is to work. You were treated excellently by everyone and the mining community was always strong. You know you was treated well by someone, when you remember their name. It was during my second week and Gary McCarthy, a man I grew to respect around the site, sent me to the stores for a long weight. Eager to please everyone, I rushed to the stores and waited patiently. What I didn't know at the time, was that there's no long weight, but a long wait for me instead. I remember standing there for ages and noticed the smirk on storeman's face, that's when I knew and went back to be laughed at. The days you had when you first started here, are the ones you remember the most. I was a young boy of seventeen when I first arrived at the Navigation Colliery, now I'm almost twenty-three. I remember the pit top's non-stop production, with drams full of coal reaching the surface and empty drams heading back down. It will be a shame emptying the buildings and watching them remove the headframes that sat above the shafts and held our gear to take us underground. I've never been in a colliery like this before, and nothing will compare to the five years I have spent here.

Stop.

After almost an hour of listening to David about his time at the Navigation Colliery, the interview has ended. I looked down to my notepad, at the first word that caught my eye; *Arabesque.*

"Did you ever watch *Arabesque*?" I asked David.

"No, I don't think I ever will. It would just remind me of what once was. It would upset me," David replied with great passion.

He stood up and had a final look around the Power House.

"There used to be two compressors over there." He pointed to the gap in the wall.

I walked David back to his car, a Ford Focus, then thanked him for his time. I watched him slowly drive away. Who knows when he will visit here again and more importantly, if he will.

Once I got home and listened to our chat, I decided to search for that scene in *Arabesque*. Luckily, I found a small snippet of the film, that featured Crumlin Viaduct in all its glory. It was proudly standing tall in the centre of a vibrant, industrial village. I found out that it closed years earlier and was in the process of being dismantled, but you could still notice its stonework and its towering span across the village. Yet, watching the clip, the Navigation Colliery only appears briefly. Its prominent red brickwork was first featured in the background, as the antagonist aimed fire from a helicopter. Next, the helicopter is shot heading towards the camera, with the Navigation Colliery featuring in the background again. You could spot the Power House, where I held my interview with David. The viaduct is featured as a disused railway bridge that the main characters ran across in a bid to escape from the antagonist. How does the film end? Gregory simply drops a wooden ladder onto the helicopter, and watches it crash into the river beneath them. After watching it myself, I'm relieved David hasn't seen it. What was featured showed the colliery in its lively and productive state. But it did not have the recognition it deserved, instead it was focussed on the innocent protagonist and blossoming romance. It was still a box-office success and caused a positive uproar in the community, but it did not reflect the beauty of a Welsh mining village. It didn't show the everlasting bonds formed by the common connection of the Navigation Colliery, it was just a small set for a large-scale production. Nothing more.

Yet to David, who I believe is now in his early seventies, saw beyond that. His memories of a strong mining community are still raw and imprinted on his mind, as if microscopic pieces of coal remained underneath his fingernails all this time.

Caragh Medlicott

Date Night

Strawberry jam is for Saturdays. I spread it thick on brown slices of toast, and it melts and mixes with the butter underneath. Rose despises this – *Butter and jam? It's like ketchup and ice cream!* – but she's not here.

It's a glowing day and I go outside with my tea and toast. The garden furniture became damp and rot-ridden long ago, so I sit on the grass cross-legged. Sometimes I sit in the park like this, smug that I'm still able to. You have to allow yourself small victories, don't you? The glare from the sun bleaches my phone screen and I'm relieved. I despise Facebook. I'm not technologically incompetent, despite what Rose would have everyone believe, but it is draining. The way I see it I have little choice in the matter; when your daughter is bad at calling but good at updating her profile picture, you take what you can.

I eat my sloppy toast with a hand poised underneath, ready to catch gunk. When jam does splatter on my palm I wipe my hand on the grass in a reflex that makes me think of Rose. Despite efforts not to, I wonder what she's doing. Most likely gobbling at a £10 fry-up in some overpriced coffee shop. I once asked her why she went to coffee shops for food, *Aren't coffee shops for coffee?* I said. *Where else would I go?* she asked. *A greasy spoon?* I suggested and it tickled her. *This isn't Corrie, Mum.*

Still, the thought of Rose gracelessly eating her bacon, spooning up beans, scraping up the last of the mushrooms – always her favourite – fills me with a carefree joy. At nineteen years old she's yet to lose her blundering girlishness. She moves and dresses without anxiety; that's rare for women. She's the only thing I'm certain I got right. After all, raising a girl is a high-wire act. You can't ban the beauty magazines, everyone knows what happens to forbidden apples. Mocking works best; teenagers are always on board for mocking.

Breakfast done, I wash up and hum off-key to the radio. I catch the ghost of my reflection in the window. She has the same sharp nose, tumbling mousy hair, but her wrinkles are lacking. Instead, her skin is all gold lines and shimmering glass. This reflection is ageless; she could be twenty, she could be sixty. There's something unbearable about it, so I walk away and wipe my hands on my jeans. There's a sticky-note on the fridge, it reads: *Sat – Rose calling at 2 for 'date do's and don'ts'*. I sigh and fold up the paper into the smallest triangle I can make then push it deep into my pocket. She'll never usually call to discuss anything, but this is the one thing I don't want to talk about and we have a time slot pencilled in.

Last night's wine bottle is still at the foot of the sofa. I bring it out to the recycling. "There is increased concern about the over-consumption of red wine in single, middle-aged mothers," I say, mimicking the newsreader I find annoying. I make a point of not remembering his name, but he looks like Rose's Dad.

Outside I see Ron – the local busy-body – jet-washing his already sparkling car. His head snaps up at the sound of the wine bottle smashing at the bottom of the wheelie bin. His frown deepens and I smile and wave at him, then retreat into the house chuckling. It's the small things.

One skill I've considerably improved since Rose left is

'pottering'. I didn't see the point of it before – who has time for watering the plants and going to the post office? But now I can potter a whole day away. I fumble along, completing mundane tasks: polishing the TV and reorganising my bookshelf, walking to the corner shop, chatting to the nice lady who works there, reading all the papers cover-to-cover, and doing the crosswords too. The phone rings at 2:15pm and I'm surprised to find that half the day has slipped away and fallen to the ground like a dropped ribbon. I click the answer button.

"Muuuuuuuuum!" Rose's voice rings in my ear, she never says hello.

"Hiya sweetie-pie."

"Ew. Mum, save all the cheese for later."

"But I do so like to use my *cheese* – as you put it – on you." She laughs. "Fine. So are you all ready?"

"Well, I'm not going for another five hours yet, so no, not really."

"You know what I mean…"

"I'm afraid I don't."

"You're so annoying." She says it with a hard 'g'.

"Thank you, darling."

I look out the kitchen window. A cat has found its way into the garden and is sunning itself on the decking.

"What are you going to wear?" she asks.

"A dress, I suppose."

"Very good. What shoes?"

"Unquestionably flats," I say. The mere thought of heels makes me shudder.

"Even better." She means it; her mother's daughter. The line goes quiet and I can't think of anything to say.

"Oh come on, Mum, talk to me."

"There's a cat in our garden," I say and hear her exhale.

"Fine," I say. "I'm nervous and I don't want to go –" I feel like a child admitting this "– I looked at his picture on the dating site again. His nose is weird and he listed Rod Stewart as one of his favourite artists. Of all time. I *hate* Rod Stewart."

"Relationships aren't founded on noses and music taste," she says.

"I know."

"Just give it a go, Mum, keep an open mind. I don't want you to be on your own."

"I know, darling."

The cat is stretched out on its back. Its black fur is like oil and its teeth glint in the sun as it yawns at the sky. I don't know how to tell Rose I'm fine on my own. I miss her, but that's not the same as loneliness.

"Hey, why don't you wear that lipstick I got you on your birthday?" she says, eager.

"You know I appreciate every present you get for me? But that lipstick, it's just very... well, very *red*."

"I know. Red suits you, that's why I got it."

"There's considerable difference between a red fleece and red lipstick," I laugh. There's muffled talking on the other end, someone saying her name.

"Mum?"

"That's me."

"I'm really sorry, I've gotta go. Text me after though, yeah?"

"Of course, go enjoy your Saturday." I'm smiling down the phone.

"Thanks Mum, good luck! Love you."

"I love you too," I say but the line's already gone dead. I keep the phone to my ear for a minute, listening to the dial tone while watching the cat, then I cut off.

I wander upstairs and into my room with the vague

intention of picking out something to wear. The curtains are closed and the room is steeped in near blackness. I feel exhaustion wash over me and a growing ache in the back of my skull. I've only had restless sleep these past weeks. My dreams have been vivid and sharp, always teetering on the edge of wakefulness.

I lie back on my bed, staying atop the covers and start with my fingers and toes. Wriggling them, then imagining them blurring. I think on a particle level; the fabric of atoms and neutrons and electrons which make up my skin and the air and the bed. It's a zooming out, more than a zooming in. I let my mind bend and stretch, only for it to snap back like an elastic band trying to fit round a basketball, I cover hardly any space – but I enjoy the effort. The topsy-turviness of it all.

This is something I used to do when I was young, a kind of thought exercise. An attempt at being philosophical – to defy or give in to existentialism – whichever liberated me more. At the time, it was about making myself feel important. Now it has the opposite effect. I have an acute awareness of my own inconsequence and it's something I find comforting. My tiny blip of consciousness, my mind, one small pocket of the universe that belongs just to me.

I sink into sleep, tiredness pressing on my chest until I go under. When I wake it's with the panic of someone who is meant to be somewhere, but it's only six and I get ready with leisure. I pick out a comfortable dress made of jumper-like material. It's black and just past the knee. Rose might call it "mumsy-ish" but this isn't an insult to me, I am a mum. I haven't worn tights in a long time and I think I've lost the art. I hitch and drag, wriggle, and pull till I'm mostly squeezed into them.

I take a last look in the mirror. Admittedly, there is some colour missing. I watch my own brows furrow with concentration as I apply the lipstick. I try, for a minute, to convince myself it works by squinting my eyes and flipping my hair, but then I rub it off. I'm only wearing it because I want a part of her with me, and she's not in the lipstick.

I'd considered attempting to survive the evening on the small amount of wine that would keep me under the driving limit... but even the thought was unbearable. I sit on the train to town surrounded by others out for the Saturday evening; couples both young and old, bare-legged girls in clattering heels and boys wearing too much hair gel and aftershave already holding cans. I see a train passing the other way and wonder what the occupiers of the carriages going out of town look like, if they're more *me*. I imagine a train full of single women, fifty-something spinsters. I only realised recently that I am – technically – a spinster. Of course, I was with Rose's dad for nearly sixteen years, but we never married. When I relayed this fact to Rose she chastised me: *Mum, don't talk like that*. Funny the overriding connotations of spinster, it has one image: Havisham. Something about the word makes me think of spiders, tangled webs and cocooned flies.

I walk to the restaurant as the day creeps away. The mixture of jumper dress and woollen tights leave me flustered and hot. By the time I get to the place – a small Italian called Murano – I have an unpleasant dampness under my arms and sweat coating my forehead, but I go in anyway. Any man who is put off by a bit of sweat can't be much fun.

I made the booking so I give the waitress my name.

"Table for two, Signora?" She has a fake Italian accent.

"Yes, thank you."

She brings me to a table with a tall candle burning and then passes me the menu. The restaurant is full but not crowded; large mirrors give the illusion of space. There is a strong smell of baked bread and the kitchen is partially exposed. Even from where I'm sat, a good few tables away, I can feel the heat from the stone oven. It drifts over like it's something tangible, stiffening the air. The waitress asks me if I'd like to wait to order drinks but I'm already pointing to the bottle of wine I want from the list on the drinks menu.

I check my watch. I was already five minutes late; cheeky perhaps, but acceptable. He's onto fifteen minutes, not a promising start. I sip at the wine and browse the menu. Each time the waitress bustles past I see her eyes flicker to me, concerned. I suspect she is worried about making me feel awkward by coming over before my date has arrived. The next time her nervous eyes graze mine I gesture her over and smile. She nods, holds up her finger, mouthing "One sec." When she returns I order a starter and she smiles, says "Good choice, Signora," and walks off. It arrives and I eat it with reverence, small savouring bites sharpened by sips of wine.

Time passes by. I see it moving like a film montage, the second hand ticking away between shots of me looking concerned and checking my phone. Except I'm not worried and I order pizza.

I cringe when the bill comes, afraid that the sweet waitress has done something awful like offer me the wine on the house. I thank the Gods she hasn't and tip her heavily. I walk out the restaurant and into the night which is filled with a fine rain, though it's only visible close to the streetlights. My phone buzzes. A message from Rose asking how it went with three winky faces all lined up next to each other at the end. I laugh and type out a reply 'Lovely! The food was wonderful too, we'll have to go sometime when you're home. Speak soon x'.

I walk down the main high street to find a taxi rank. A group of drunk boys walk past and one of them wolf-whistles at me. I laugh at him and stick my tongue out. The wooden heels of my boots click on the pavement, but not like the stilettos of the girls on the train; this is a heavy, clanking sound. A black cab zooms down the road with his yellow light on and I manage to hail it. As the car pulls in the headlights shoot white in my eyes, blinding me for a moment. I walk to the car, feeling my shadow grow out behind me; long and dark. The taxi door slams shut.

"Where to?" asks the driver.

"Home," I say, then give him my address. The taxi drives out of town, past the lights and noise, people and bustle, till Saturday night has all fallen away and we're back in the suburbs.

Eve Moriarty

Kaunas

i. Everyone I know is being cut open in the morning

My best friend
speaks no English, so we
pantomime our way through blood
tests and bumpy drives
on potholed roads.
My feet are birds. Juddering
with nerves, they flutter
the anxious rotation
of an anti-clotting
exercise.
Before the clinic,
I am smiling too much
at cashiers, waitstaff, two hours
ahead of home and marooned
in the future.
Skyping home, I reach back
through time and pull
my mother towards me
through hostel Wi-Fi.

ii. Pain makes me Catholic

The night I
go under I dream my
Spanish roommate is saying
a Rosary, pressing the cross
into my hand hard
enough for blood.

I wake to needles,
checks and tests until
I am a three of swords, each
hot point of pain holding
me inside my skin.
I start to heal.

I relearn speech, walk
on Bambi limbs as eager
for praise as an infant.

iii. Everything is simple

Women feed us pills and
put us to bed. One night the nurse
rests her hand, warm
and human on my bandaged chest.

We all pretend we want to leave.

Saoirse O'Connor

The Early Bird

It seemed like the rain in the city was constant. It hammered down, or spat, or remained half way between the two relentlessly. The inhabitants lived with their collars up, and umbrellas at their fingertips as easily as they breathed. Rain was not remarked upon but accepted as part of the bargain to live in a city where everything was walkable, where the green spaces were numerable, where children rode their bikes safely and perhaps most importantly for the residents of Cathays, the price of a pint was at least a third cheaper than that of their London counterparts.

It was this last Welsh bounty that had led Matt to stumble home, just as dawn decided to make itself known over the rooftops on a typically wet Wednesday morning. The bins had been put out for collection the night before, and the seagulls had risen early. Perhaps not to catch the worm, but instead the last remaining beans that clung to the tins inside the plastic sacks. Combined with the chips and fried chicken that littered the streets from the previous evening, the gulls' breakfast resembled the more decadent feasts of the kings who had once inhabited the many castles in the nearby countryside. As such, Matt kicked his way through old newspapers, empty cans of Fosters, and the other gently rotting detritus that marked Cathays firmly within the borders of a student shanty town.

The blessings of an already cheap pint combined with a student card were now beginning to sour. As Matt struggled to recollect the events of the night before that had turned a quick drink into a long and most likely expensive night in the many pubs, bars and clubs of Cardiff, he equally struggled to recognise if this was, in fact, his road. Like so many of the streets that made up this particular area of the city, it looked much the same to outsiders, and on occasion, to its own drunken residents. Nearly identikit houses stood packed with as many students as would put up with its overcrowded and rubbish-strewn streets, its callous and greedy landlords, and the many screeching seagulls that were not only loud but occasionally violent. The pubs were littered liberally across the streets and made it almost criminally easy to hop, as Matt had done the previous evening, from one closing to another till the virtues of the student discount were nearly as moot as the probability of making it to lectures in the morning. As he finally recognised and reached his own front door, Matt briefly thought of his bank account and shuddered. His key finally turning in the lock, he passed thankfully into his own hall, up to his own bed, and finally into the welcome dark of oblivion.

When he finally awoke, the dawn had not only receded but vanished completely. Instead the world outside was lit only by the neon orange of the street lamps, and the curious white light of the half-moon that hung absent-mindedly above. Matt's whole body shouted at him, as he blearily looked for what had pulled him from sleep. The hammering on the door that had awoken him was slowly building to a crescendo, and it took Matt several attempts to locate and pull on tracksuit bottoms before heaving his aching body downstairs. One of the joys of reading week meant that Matt had the run of the house, his housemates having gone home to meals cooked by other people, beds made by other people, bringing with them bags of laundry to be washed by someone else. Unfortunately, being the only person in the house meant that there was no one else to open doors to overenthusiastic strangers.

"Yes?"

The awkward faces of what was clearly a house viewing gazed back at him, some of them shuffling their feet out of cold or awkwardness. Matt groaned inwardly. Sam had mentioned something about people coming to look at the house.

"Just keep it tidy, mate, the landlord's been getting a bit shirty about how long it's taking to get new people in."

Matt took a swift look over his shoulder. It wasn't that the house was untidy exactly, more an overall feeling of grubbiness. Counters had a vague stickiness to them that transferred to your hands when you touched them, old magazines were piled haphazardly so the pull-outs and supplements spilled onto the table. The washing up on the side was clean enough but it was normally best to give the spoon a wipe before using it to stir your tea. All in all, it was exactly what should be expected of a student house.

The girl at the front of the little group cleared her throat. "Hi, is it ok if we come in and take a look around?"

Matt nodded and stepped aside to let them in, suddenly aware of his naked chest. He legged it upstairs, waving a hand behind him to signal he'd be back down momentarily. The group loitered at the bottom of the stairs, the bravest of them peering into the living room where packaging and boxes were arranged like offerings around the giant TV which took up the majority of one wall. The only jumper Matt could find was his sports club hoodie which had a suspicious dark stain down the front; he shoved it on. 'Oh well,' he thought, 'they won't be here for long.'

Matt walked downstairs slowly. His head was banging, and he really just wanted to go to bed. He wondered if the best thing to do would be to go and slowly make a cup of tea, while They (they had already converged into a homogenous mass inside his head) stared into the vacant rooms of his friends, marvelling at the mess that only a houseful of boys with no mother could make. His own room was no better than any of the others, clothes littered the floor, condoms and lube spilled over his desk with more regularity than any of the books he was meant to be reading, and a look in the bin would have revealed a startling number of empty boxes from the chippy that it was a rule he passed on his way home from a night out.

He put the kettle on and sat awkwardly at the kitchen table as he listened to them bumbling around the house. The ache in his head grew suddenly worse when he got up to get a mug and the teabags, and he knew suddenly with the utmost confidence that he was about to vomit. With one hand covering his mouth he ran clumsily to the toilet and was sick until retching brought up only violent yellow bile that made his entire body recoil. It was only after sitting up and leaning his forehead against the cold of the bathtub, that he realised the house viewers had been inspecting the shower room next door. He heard a girl, he thought the one from the landlord, saying something to the others before they seemed to move off upstairs. Dammit. If they were upstairs, he couldn't make a swift exit to his room, the thought of seeing them on the stairs made him squirm. He had always hated being sick as a child, the thought of strangers hearing the result of his excesses the night before made him feel sick all over again.

"Hi. Sorry, but you sounded like you needed this." The girl from before was standing over him, offering a mug of tea. Dazed, Matt accepted. It was hot and sweet and the waves in his stomach settled a little.

"Thanks." He took another sip. "Bit of a long one last night," Matt offered sheepishly. The girl waved her hand.

"Please. No need to tell me, feel like I've seen the SU under strobe lighting more than I've seen it in daylight." She nodded towards the kitchen. "I've told them to have a look around without me, that I'll be in the kitchen if they have any questions, if you fancy a chat?" She walked out, and Matt was left clutching the mug like it would somehow help him up from the bathroom floor.

When he finally had managed to uncurl his body and make his way shakily to the kitchen, he found her sat at the table lazily swiping on her phone.

Matt joined her somewhat awkwardly and fiddled with the mug.

"You been doing this long?" he asked to fill the silence. She looked up from her phone and smiled.

"No, not long."

"Is it just house viewings you do? Or like paperwork and stuff as well?"

She smiled again. "Yeah. Something like that." She went back to her phone. Matt found himself getting annoyed. This was still his house, and she was the one who had asked him for a chat. He sat looking at the teabag she'd left in the mug. The final dregs of tea tasted more like tea leaves, almost earthy, but he drank them anyway.

"You don't recognise me, do you?" she said, a hint of what could have been bemusement or frustration in her voice. Matt shook his head.

"No. Um, sorry."

"The first night out in Freshers last year. You took me back to your room in Taly."

Suddenly, Matt did remember her. The awkward laughter as they had tried to manoeuvre on the tiny toddler sized bed, before he had dramatically swept the stuff off his desk and lifted her onto it. How after she'd pulled the blankets off his bed and they'd curled up on the floor, how he'd whispered to her how terrified he'd been leaving home. How this had made it all a little bit better. How he hadn't called her the next day.

"Ah. Sorry. Again," he said. "You know how Freshers is."

"Yeah," she replied frostily, "one girl out the next one in, right?"

"Nah, just all a bit overwhelming you know." He looked up at her, and her blue eyes seemed to soften for a second.

"I guess. It's just not the best feeling when a one-night stand forgets you exist." She had stopped playing with her phone now. "I mean," she corrected, "when your first one-night stand forgets you exist."

It wasn't just Matt's hangover that was making his stomach churn now. "Well, is your number still the same?" he ventured. "Maybe I could make it up to you? Maybe not just for the one night this time?"

She looked at him for a moment, then laughed. "Yeah, shoot me a message if you want to get in touch."

"Or maybe I'll see you around here again?"

"No," she said decisively, "I normally only come to a house once."

"Ah. Just that good huh?"

"Yeah," she said. "Something like that." Her phone beeped, and she glanced at it. She peered past Matt down the hall and nodded. "On that note, I think we should leave you in peace. I'll see you around, Matt." She put her phone in her pocket and started to walk down the hall to the door.

"Wait!" Matt called after her. "What's your name?"

"Whatever's in your phone I guess," she shouted. Matt heard the door click and smiled. He put his mug in the sink and decided to go back to bed, he'd go through his phone in the morning. Maybe send her a cheeky message about viewings.

As he walked past the living room, he noticed the TV wasn't on the wall, and hadn't he left his phone on the table in there? He stood for a second, confused, then jumped when someone started knocking on the door. He opened it, still puzzled. There was a small group gathered on the doorstep led by a man Matt vaguely recognised as his landlord.

"Hi, we're here for a house viewing. Sam should have said something about a group coming around?"

Morgan Owen

Connecting Journey Chester

Blue-lit dawn through a train window
greying at the edges
walking the shadow-green
over fallow and dusty yards
blinking into life; and across the grey
a split of orange, watery:
washed flame in ash. The morning
glows on the worn-smooth rails.

Dowlais Dream

Love in the pale glint at morning
and the down of thistles
scattered in the dewed fields;
it is here, to this salient of green
needling along the road
and the backs of terraces
that I return in dreams: to Dowlais.
A faint musty smell hangs
about the frontier farms
keened with pine in a northern
breeze rounding the soles
of a saddled mountain.
The birches almost bare
and a sharpness in the air
suggests snow; on this ridge
I can see my home
and all the traces of my journeys
through margins and broken places
and the oak woods tenacious
in hollows and deeply cut nooks
on the mountainside. I can see
the standing-stoned
and cairned tops and the village
winding down towards
the town on the valley floor.
The steel no longer sings
but all my worlds
converge upon me in this high place.

Gelligaer Common

The dreaming stone and the glaucous seed:
someone's left the moon
in the reeds
on the edge of the common.
Split light in the cold furrows;
fragments of ghost frost
vein the coarse mountain grass.
Only the far-off hum of cars
and a faint orange glow
remind you there's a town
somewhere beyond the dark.

All time was an owl's eye
watching the plain below
run green to fallow,
then to ice,
like impudent men who leave
their names in stone to splinter
in the moonlit night.
Nowhere is the silence
before and after a fleeting song.

Rhea Seren Phillips

The Copse Candles[1]

From the copse, the *Deer* stared breathless
and claimed the heart of me; deathless
with anticipation, I yawned
livid flesh, rived arteries; dawned
canu. Lobomised its truth;
Tylwyth Teg[2] stole a cream tooth-
the essence of nitrate myth.
Flesh stretched, spliced and aching, yet pith
against the constraint of the hoar.
Turn to the devil at your door;
Deer ruminates the septum's cud,
newt draws an isopleth through mud
and realigns this strange distance.
Deer mutters to non-existence.

---

[1] Poetic form: cyhydedd fer. The poem's title is a play on 'corpse', referring to the corpse candles of Aberglasney Gardens. It also refers to a deer's eye lying in a copse.

[2] "Tylwyth Teg" are small Welsh goblins commonly known for their mischievous tricks.

Jack Rendell

The Flump King's Quest

Somewhere in the woods where the Flump King troods
and the tubby-nucks gibble and run,
a fairy sings with her glimmer-trim wings
shining in the morning sun.

'Flump King! Flump King, hear me sing!
Take a pause in your trample-dash walk.
Your buttercup face and your daydream mace
are needed for magical work!

'Go to the rocks where the kappa tick-tocks
and the damplings robble in the treed.
Wander and dance in the riverside plants,
snow feet tickling the reeds.

'My notes will race and your sunrise face
will shine down the riddle-back dale,
scattering the wraiths to the thistledown place
as the shadowlace banshees wail.

'Under the vines, the Ruby Dwarf mines
rever with a rufescent gleam.
Greet the royal train of fire-pick maids
and offer your mace of dreams.

'Place it on a sheet at the Ruby Queen's feet.
She will smile with her living-gem lips.
She'll lift it, hold it, exhale and fill it
with the joys of a thousand sleeps.

'Take yourself then to the eldergleam glen
where the crow king's head lives on.
Hear him tell of the border-rim bell
glowing in the velvetine sun.

'Travel to the place where the ooji-burrs chase
and the snoobulence gallops in the groves.
The great bell gleams with an aureate sheen
as it senses you come close.

'As the end-day bleeds, rise like a steed.
Strike it with the daydream mace.
The note will swell and like a diamond crab's shell,
will shatter and its music cease.

'And by your hand, this delicious land
shall be rent from the mortal realm,
never to be seen, but for in a dream.
Like a long in the hearts of men.'

Laura Mae Satterthwaite

Ecstasy

You telling me:
I'm sorry for your loss
Doesn't dull the blow
Or soften the ache.

My pain won't be lessened with
Time passing
Or your god forbidden
Blessings of *she's in a better place.*

Her better place was
Moulded in my arms.
Fingers intertwined,
A complete jigsaw puzzle
Desperate to collapse.

Perfectly imperfect.

How could I bear to live
Without her bottle blue eyes
Dragging me back to a time
where things were oh so simple.

Intoxicated on £3 wine
High on ecstasy.
We were a pair of crazed doves
Soaring through the air

My drug came not as a pill
Or a powder.
My ecstasy came
In the sweet curves
of her smile.

Gareth Smith

Closed Book

They lied about the baby's mother, of course. Everybody knew, but that wasn't the point. It wasn't so much about whether they were telling the truth – because it was bloody obvious they weren't – but about whether they were respectable enough for it to be believed.

It happened all the time. Wedding dates were moved back in order to accommodate inconvenient births. Mentally ill relatives were erased from existence if they'd done something particularly violent or unpleasant. It didn't matter that the bride was pregnant on her wedding day, or that we'd spotted the blood-soaked handprint on the ambulance door. It mattered whether the people lying were good and honest folk.

If they were, we all held hands and believed the untruth together like any other Sunday in church. If they weren't, if they failed the means test of respectability, then we refused to chant their hymn and they were cast out into the cold, harsh light of truth. I often wondered how one could measure 'respectability', but I never got a helpful definition. It seemed it was a little, flexible putty that could be moulded depending on whose hands it was in. It might change a little, so long as the shape could still be recognised.

It's funny, really. Change is the one thing I didn't count on.

I started collecting secrets as a child. I had so little else. A different little boy, always perceiving vaguely that there was a secret list of expectations for me and that I was, unknowingly, always acting against them. The type of boy that the others don't like, or turn against suddenly, the sort that women pity initially and then are suddenly irritated by.

I spent a lot of time with my mother and her friends, patronised but rarely consulted. A collection of local married and widowed women who wore housecoats and pinnys, smoked with their curlers in and continually claimed they 'wouldn't be able to stop' as mornings were whiled away in our front room. Conversation rarely varied. We – or, rather, they – spoke of people.

People we knew. People they knew. People we didn't know and shouldn't wish to. The people that peopled the streets, pubs and shops in our council estate maze. It was a network, a patchwork and we were all overlapping with one another via fascinating, hidden threads. Learning of connections – good ones and bad ones – gave me a strange thrill of proximity to everyone. I felt a little less lonely as I saw us all intertwined.

Some of the information was benign. Marriages, births and deaths – like a registry, Mam's was – but I enjoyed the warm, cosy feeling that they engendered. This was harmless chatter, background information, it certainly wasn't gossip. The latter (which is never idle, by the way) started to take my fancy as I got older.

Amid the announcements of welcome pregnancies and dignified deaths, stodgy and a little stale, juicier stories occasionally emerged. Whispered in a breathy hurry and accompanied by nervous glances in my direction, I started to learn about the shadows that outlined the figures on our street. I heard that Mr. Jenkins and Mrs. George continued their affair with increasing nonchalance, but the real tragedy was that Mrs. Jenkins knew and used alcohol to mask the pain. I learnt that Mr. Spooner had not died of a burst appendix but of drinking bleach and the horrible truth of his death was being desperately concealed from his children. Sandra Porter was caught in the backseat of a car with a man twice her age. Henry Watkins was stealing from the Con Club's coffers.

I consumed these tidbits ravenously. I got greedy. One day, I made the mistake of contributing. They were discussing Mrs. Ridley, who wasn't actually pregnant at all, but awkwardly covering for her teenage daughter. I thought about this a little and ventured forward. My childish, feminine voice cut into the stuffy air and scraped against it.

"Won't they notice she hasn't got a big belly too?"

Heads turned as if only just noting my presence. My mother's smile set suddenly as though her face had been pickled in aspic. I was pushed out of the room with a cold hand and a word of muttered apology. Once the guests were gone, she started screaming. I absorbed the shame with wet eyes and reddening cheeks and I knew my time had come to an end.

That didn't stop me, of course. It just made me smarter about the whole business. I was learning the value of the word 'secret', of its power as ammunition against the secrets of others. I began to listen more carefully to what people said, to pay attention to the gaps and omissions as well as the loud and boorish chatter. As should be obvious, what people don't say is far more revealing than what they do. I started opening the post when I could get my hands on it, listening in to phone calls and hiding in hallways and alleys to eavesdrop.

It was a type of moral education. I learnt what was right or wrong by whether or not it was a secret. I remember overhearing that the grocer's son had been questioned by a policeman after being 'caught' in the local park's toilets. I hoarded that secret for quite a few years before I realised exactly what he could've done in those grubby toilets that was so appalling. When I finally understood, it only hardened my resolve.

Gradually, the times changed. The nature of the secrets changed with them. Divorce, once a highly valued nugget of scandal, lost its lustre. Premarital pregnancy was bled of its shame, mental illness exchanged embarrassed silence for defiant compassion. Certain stories found their currency freefalling and disappeared from circulation altogether. Of course, not everything disappeared. In our backward little back streets, the likes of addictions and same-sex affairs were still to be sneered at. I spent my adolescent years ready to use my secrets when necessary, massaging them gently like a loaded gun in my pocket. The children I had played with became adults and had children of their own. The chattering circle that had gathered in our front room dwindled, flickered and disappeared. Mam was one of the last to go, trapped in the front room in a hospital bed and craning her neck to look out into an empty street.

Decades later and things are unrecognisable. Most of the people behind the locked doors and closed curtains are strangers and their secrets are unobtainable. They talk and type on their phones, flickering and clicking their tablets and laptops. That's where the hidden lives are found these days. Digital secrets, away from the street and inside the screen. Too late for me. That's when I had the idea of writing them down. It felt like a sudden purge before the end, a desire to watch them all spill out before they left their container for good. I bought a cheap spiral notebook from the closest discount shop and scribbled every secret I could remember inside. From the haziest of my childhood memories to the most recent meagre scraps, I committed every one to paper in a slow, arthritic scrawl.

Long-dead names, inscribed for the first time in decades, were resurrected for a brief respite. Events from the forgotten past resurfaced on the page; my fingers tingled with their dying power. I wrote my own name last, ostentatiously looping each *O* and allowing the final *S* to curl into a high-kick. I wrote my own secrets in full details, pushing the pen into the final full stop until it looked like congealed blood.

My instinct was to throw it into the fire. Melodramatic, but impractical. A little bit like me. The open fire went out decades ago. I racked my brain to think of the most appropriate ritual to dispose of them, drawing a blank until I remembered the rusty barbecue in the garden shed. I trudged outside, opened the door with a feeble tug of the latch, and allowed the mildew to envelop my senses. I dragged the blackened globe across the tile on rickety legs and, through sheer willpower, managed to light it again.

I'd begun ripping the first pages for incineration when I heard a voice.

"What are you doing?"

The little girl from next door. She was balancing precariously on something at the other side of our dividing wall.

"I'm having a barbecue."

She pushed herself a little further up, balancing on tiptoes. "I love barbecue sauce and ribs. Are you making that?"

Before I could answer, her father appeared with bin bags in his hand.

"Get down from there. She's not bothering you, is she?"

Like a spark, conversation ignited. The wife came out and we all agreed what a shame it was that neighbours didn't speak anymore. The couple on the other side, watering their plants, joined in and agreed with added enthusiasm. A suggestion was proffered that, seeing as we were having such lovely weather, we organise a street barbecue for Saturday evening. Ask as many people as possible and BYOB!

Against all odds, that's exactly what happened. At least ten homes from the street participated. I was among them, making banal conversation with the adults while the children ran in circles around us. Cheeseburgers and cheap wine were consumed, old CDs blasted from even older players. It was the closest thing to community I've felt there in years. I heard a few people talk about me, mentioning 'he's lived here his whole life' and 'looked after his mother – they were very close'. I felt a warm glow inside.

I'm glad I didn't burn that notebook. As the sky darkened and the alcohol flowed, the air became a breeding ground for secrets. They hadn't gone away at all. They'd been lying dormant, I suppose, awaiting fresh opportunities. I certainly didn't waste any time, collecting a respectable amount from slurred lips or furtive glances at bright screens. The evening ended with promises to do something similar soon. I shall need to invest in some new notebooks.

*

'They lied about the baby's mother, of course'. I've got a photo of her pasted at the back of the notebook – the elder 'sister' sent away to live with relatives shortly after I was born. She looks young, pretty and stupid – everything that I imagine that she was. Dead ten years later in a car accident. Mam keeping the secret until five days before she died.

No wonder I should've been so drawn to secrets. I've been one from the moment I was born.

Samuel Verdin

The Tools of my Trade

The Head Waiter of Le Plume is a man named Long. Long is rope-bound and wound tight into a black waistcoat and a lengthy white apron. He elegantly glides amongst the tables situated within the restaurant's main floor (Heave! Ho! Heave! Ho!). The room is crimson and dignified and the hooks of its walls hold portraits of cultural titans and a couple of dogs. The floor's centre raises a pianist named Monica, playing upon a small, circular stage. Her legs and arms are a murmur, for it is known that humans are still humans and not piano keys and the keys of Monica's piano believe that they are unfeeling machines; limbs muted in their raw material.

She smiles to Long as he passes.

Long looks to her arched back.

She straightens her posture.

Long is not a nice man.

*

TABLE I

Two children sitting between two empty seats. They are innocent, available and without supervision. Both are wearing T-shirts portraying different characters rearing to

165

charge. One hero. One villain. And the children will follow these enemies until they're old enough to follow themselves.

Whilst reaching into his pocket for a pen the tips of Long's fingers play, out of sight, only to be found shortly after covered in ink. 'Bien,' he thought, 'ma memoire devra faire,' and with that his memory wipes the sleep from its eyes, rolls out of bed and puts the kettle on, rather annoyed.

"Bonsoir, Monsieur, Madame! Aimerez-vous voir le menu des vins?"

Inside Long laughs and leans his head back displaying to anyone who happens to look a condescending grin. The children stare up. Their eyes begin to tear.

No experience that these children have had could ever answer for why Long smiled in such a way. This left them in his mind without trial, as naked and fruitless as the branches of November.

His memory sips at its tea whilst one of the children weeps. The second child asks for a tissue as Long drifts over to the next table (Heave! Ho!).

*

ALMOST THERE…

Between these tables
Long longed to
fill,
happened a small,

               slight

inconvenience.
One that
he nor
I

had expected.
A glass of
average size
fell to the crimson,
s h a t t e r i n g
into a
million,
billion,
trillion pieces everywhere and unfortunately for Long he shrieked and all the portraits in the room had worried faces and fear swept across him, drowned him, frowned him and pushed him into the back of the room along with all of the other wasted imaginings of what people may say, think, do, whisper, giggle, judge, preach and wonder, and all this would happen under the thunder of Monica's keys, unfeeling and ruthless and why, he would ask me, would I make such a thing happen when he believes to be a Sancho to me as I a Don to him and I would say,
Shhh…
My poor Long.
Everything
is
going to be OK.
Imagine,
just *imagine*,
that every
single
person
in the room
is naked,
and you are not.

*

TABLE II

Long gathers himself from amongst the shards of glass and makes his way to the next table, passing a judgemental glance to an old woman – left completely naked (and careless to it) and at the mercy of Long's imagination – her cracked, low skin and the purple veins around her ankles. The portraits rest and resume their pose: the dogs looking up to a man holding a pheasant, heroically, and the rounded faces of white women sit above their blown-up gowns, a look of unwarranted decency held in their eyes.

As he passes, a junior waiter asks a blushed, rounded giant with an expensive tooth if she can get him or the two much younger ladies on either side of him anything. He asks for the bill and she hands it to him, expecting this response.

"I don't suppose we can pay in innocence, can we?" asks the bear, coughing a laugh over the table with two feminine hands placed on either side of his chest.

At the second table sits a writer, a critic, casually swirling, smelling and sipping his wine. One leg rests over the knee of the other. One hand holds his glass. One hand holds a pen independently noting anything that occurs.

"Monsieur, is everything OK with the wine?" Long asks.

"Yes," the man replies. "I'm ready to order."

"And what will you be having this evening, monsieur?"

"The lamb."

"Ah…" A look of memorable pleasure slides across Long's lips until one corner peaks. His memory rubs its hands together in excitement. "An *ex*cellent choice, monsieur…"

Long takes the menu, bows, ever so slightly, pauses for a moment and gives the order to the kitchen through a door just to the left of the table.

*

THE ELDERLY WOMAN – PART I

Moments later, several metres from the critic's table, the elderly woman is speaking with Long. The critic's hand and pen work in ultimate unison as his eyes survey the silent conversation. It lasts for one minute and thirty-three seconds. As the service bell rings in the kitchen, demanding Long's attention, the critic's left ear turns to face the door.

*

KITCHEN, FROM THE CRITIC'S EAR

VOICE 1: I told you! We don't have enough fucking lamb!

LONG: You never mentioned anything, putain!

VOICE 1: I did!

VOICE 2: We only have five, Chef, and they're taken by the pre-order.

VOICE 1: Fool! Who is it for?

LONG: I believe it is for the infamous Jacque Burdon.

VOICE 3: The *critic*?!

LONG: Oui…

VOICE 1: FOOL!

A moment of silence passes.

VOICE 1: It'll take time. He'll have to wait thirty minutes… James!

VOICE 3: Oui, Chef?

VOICE 1: Tell reception to call the party and see if we can change one lamb.

VOICE 3: Oui, Chef.

*

THE ELDERLY WOMAN – PART II

The elderly woman sits at her table using her varnished lips to skin a mouthful of crème brûlée from a spoon. Her appearance leaves no secrets to the imagination, concealing only her organs. The candle on her table flickers a little as the critic approaches her, his right hand resting in the palm of the other behind his back. A friendly expression warms his face as she looks up to him, polite but indifferent.

"Madame," he nods.

She swallows. The critic hears it go down. "Good evening, young man."

"May I ask, if it is not too rude, what it was that you spoke of with the waiter? Pardon me, I am an inquisitive soul, you see…"

"Oh, I don't mind. Nothing really. He wanted to ask why I wasn't wearing any clothes."

"I see… And, if you don't mind such an interrogation, why aren't you?"

"Well," she chuckles to herself, looking down at her dessert with artificial patience before returning her attention to the man. "If I'm honest, I was about to ask you the same question."

"Oh, really?" replies the critic.

"Well, of course," she continues. "You're writing about all of us, aren't you?"

*

NOTES:
Fear: 12.48% of this text focuses on Long's embarrassment –

an inaccurate representation of Long's insecurity as he is generally considered to be rather worried about a lot of things. But we weren't talking about fear then. We are now.

39.2% of Long's daily mental and physical reactions are due to fear. Coincidentally, this is the same percentage of Long's French dialogue and his French heritage (his grandfather lost an arm in the war – Heave! Ho! Heave! Ho!).

Here are Long's daily fears in chronological order: Fear of bad breath; fear of missing a spot; fear of being hit by a car; fear of James Farrelli; fear of forgetting; fear of never being pictured on the walls of Le Plume, fear of choking; fear of dropping something; fear of uncontrollable bodily functions; fear of a change in sexual appetite and the social ramifications; fear of his junior colleagues' failing to perform their duties to a satisfactory level; fear of being blamed; fear of alcohol; fear of being hit by a car; fear of slipping in the shower; fear of leaving something on; fear of swallowing a spider during his sleep; fear of being forgotten.

Josh Weeks

Dougie

He looked how Colonel Kurtz would have looked if he'd made it out of the jungle: overweight; eyes of a zealot; the wisps around his bald spot tied into the limpest of ponytails.

'Bastard!' he screamed at the landlord. 'You cheeky, jobsworth bastard.'

His empty Fosters glass was already in smithereens on the other side of the lounge. 'Forty years I've been coming here, and you wanna have me barred for this?'

He pointed to the translucent bag of prawn crackers sitting on the bar.

'I've told you a thousand times, Doug – you can't bring food in here.'

Mark stepped out from behind the bar with a broom in one hand, a pint of cider and black in the other. He'd only been at The Golden Foal for six months or so, but seeing as he was barely thirty, and this was his first taste of responsibility since leaving the Wetherspoons in Ebbw Vale, he hadn't taken long to put his stamp on the place.

'Well, where do you expect me to go then? The non-pol's shut down – The Dagmar's full of kids…'

'You should have thought of that before you started throwing glasses.'

'C'mon – one more chance, mun.'

Mark arced his way past Dougie as if avoiding a landmine. 'I gave you one more chance last week.'

'No you never… what was it about?'

'That's half your problem, Doug – you're getting so wasted these days you can't even remember what you've done.'

It wasn't anything bad, as far as misdemeanours go. He'd cheated on the Thursday quiz; robbed the winners of a £20 food voucher. To be fair, Dougie had been relatively well behaved since Mark arrived, and Mark, in turn, had treated him like any other customer. But word travels fast in a town of 15,000: the street fights; the time spent in the jail; the military; the dead dog. The moment Dougie's glass shattered against the back wall, so did Mark's conviction that all of these stories were exaggerated.

'You've got a month till you can come back in,' said Mark. 'But Mark…'

'I'm not gonna change my mind, Doug.'

Dougie's scowl fell away; his eyes began to fill up. When he finally gave in after another ten minutes of pleading, he settled on a curb outside and finished his Chinese alone.

*

The first time he tries coffee is like the first time he tried whisky: it makes him wince, burns his throat, and then leaves him feeling sick for the next half hour. The whisky was when he was twelve years old; searching through his mother's kitchen cabinet whilst she was out working at the office. Now, it's a caramel latte, in the precinct block by the cenotaph that used to belong to Peacocks.

He glances around at the burgundy walls; the padded wall-seats; the women with their hair tied-up. He's been to a fair few cafes in his time, but never to one of these coffee chains that have been popping up throughout the town over the last few years. At Penny's he'd order a mug of tea and a special breakfast; it's only 50p per extra item, so he'd ask for his beans to be separated from the rest by a mound of black pudding and a galley of hash browns. But since he's with Mrs. Donnelly today, and he'd insisted that she be the one to choose where they went, he keeps his craving for a fry-up to himself and lets her do the ordering.

'Two large caramel lattes' – she turns away from the young girl behind the counter who's taking her order. 'They're bloody beautiful. I'd usually go medium but today I just can't help it.'

'Anything to eat with that, Madame?'

She swings back to the girl. 'To eat? Oh I dunno… I don't want to be greedy. What d'you say, Dougie?'

He looks at the array of treats behind the pane of glass in front of him. A piece of dense chocolate cake catches his eye.

'Granola bars,' she says without asking him. 'Two granola bars please – I'll tell you Doug, they're the new thing, you're gonna love 'em.'

He watches the girl – from what he can see on her apron she's got a foreign name, Barista – take a pair of tongs and put what looks like two rectangles of condensed rabbit food onto a plate with some napkins. After a palaver with a card and something about points, they finally make it to a table.

*

He first met Mrs. Donnelly not long after the prawn cracker debacle. He'd spent his first couple of nights standing at the bar in The Dagmar, but the prices have gone up since Barry Lennon died, and he couldn't handle the youngsters who cornered the jukebox and bombarded the place with music he hated prior to even hearing it. After losing his temper over a curry-night deal that didn't include Fosters, he gave up and bought a six-pack from the off-license to drink at home.

'Bastard junk-mail,' he muttered, kicking away the stack of unopened envelopes that had built up in the doorway. He balanced his takeaway bag on the radiator and gathered them in his arms like a reluctant uncle. The envelope at the top of the pile was from the Universal Credit scheme, but he put his thumb over the "Urgent" tab and threw the whole lot into the storage cupboard where he kept his shoes.

He didn't have Sky – he didn't even have Freeview – but he did have a small collection of VCRs stacked up beside the TV. Most of them he bought back in the eighties; movies he'd watched so many times that the tape inside has begun to disintegrate. Marlon Brando was the running theme – he had *Mutiny on the Bounty*, *The Island of Dr. Moreau*, *Last Tango in Paris*, and *Apocalypse Now*. He'd spent countless hours at The Foal arguing that the latter is better than the first two *Godfather* films put together.

He woke to the sunlight gleaming through the window; the remnants of his sweet n sour chicken congealed on a plate beside him. An image of Lieutenant Kilgore was jittering on the TV screen, and after a moment of confusion, he remembered putting on *Apocalypse Now* before he fell asleep.

He heard his doorbell ring. His doorbell *never* rang. He rubbed his eyes and got to his feet, but it felt as if an anchor had been dropped somewhere inside him. By the time he'd dragged himself to the door, the bell had rung at least three times.

'Hold your bastard horses,' he said. 'The lock's a friggin' pain to open.'

'No worries, love,' he heard a female voice reply.

He stopped what he was doing for a second. 'I'm sorry, who is it?'

'Mrs. Donnelly, from downstairs,' the voice replied. 'These blokes from Universal Credit were round here looking for you yesterday.'

He opened the door and saw Mrs. Donnelly standing there: a short, roundish woman with shutter-slits for eyes, and hair as grey as cigarette ash.

'Did they say what they wanted?' he asked, checking to see if his ponytail was still in place.

'No, they didn't – but they said that it was important that you got in touch…'

He knew perfectly well why they're looking for him, as it happens. He'd been doing a bit of side work loading cars onto a ship down at the docks, and the staff at the job centre had warned him that if he didn't let them know when he started earning money he'd be committing benefit fraud, and risk being arrested. But Dougie being Dougie, he'd pissed off a co-worker by stealing his packed lunch. It looked like his threat wasn't an empty one, after all.

'Well, cheers for letting me know,' he said, beginning to close the door.

'Wait – do you like corned beef pie?'

Dougie stared at Mrs. Donnelly blankly.

'It's just I made one a couple of days ago, and with my appetite, it's only going to go to waste.'

She wrung her hands together and looked at him nervously, as if waiting for a piece of news that could alter the course of her life.

'Aye…I s'pose I'll have it if it's just going in the bin.'

'Great,' she said. 'I'll just pop down and grab it for you now.'

She rushed down the stairs and left Dougie standing in

the doorway, the patter of her footsteps echoing through the hall. When she returned with an anaemic-looking pie missing only a sliver, he cracked the slightest of smiles, and said he'd better get ready for work.

*

'What do you think of the coffee, then? I'll tell you what, you should try dipping your granola bar in.'

Dougie does his best to hide his displeasure and tells her it's great – that he's finally been converted. He can't stomach the thought of another bite of the granola bar, but he dips it in anyway, and hopes for a miracle.

'That's the one,' she says. 'It sucks up the coffee see.'

He takes a gulp and slowly brings it back up to the surface, but as he starts pulling it towards his mouth, half the bar breaks away, and ends up in pieces on the floor.

She laughs the laugh he's grown used to over these past few weeks – a laugh that begins in fits and starts, before gradually exploding beyond her control.

*

A few days after the corned beef pie she brought him a tin of Welsh cakes, which was followed by some mackerel; a trifle; a shepherd's pie. Mrs. Donnelly, he thought, must have no sense of proportion when it comes to cooking – everything she brought him had hardly been touched, and he started to wonder whether he'd ever have to cook for himself again.

But the Wednesday of that week she didn't turn up. Initially Dougie was annoyed. He'd become so accustomed to having Mrs. Donnelly bring him his dinner that he hadn't even been to the supermarket, and had nothing to eat in the house. But as he was making his way out of the flat to go to the Chinese takeaway, his annoyance turned to curiosity, and before he knew it, to concern.

He knocked on her door. 'Mrs. Donnelly... is everything okay?' At first there was no response, and he guessed that she must have been out. But just as he turned to leave the building he heard the softest of muffling, and then her voice. 'Dougie? Is that you? I've had a fall, Dougie – and I couldn't reach the phone...'

'I'm coming now,' he shouted, rushing outside. Luckily, Mrs. Donnelly lived on the ground floor, so after fishing for a brick in a skip on the other side of the street, he smashed her living room window and threw himself clumsily over the threshold.

'I'm in the bathroom, Doug!'

He followed her voice through a tiny hallway that was identical to his own, bar the array of photographs that lined the wall. Most of them were of two young girls that he assumed were her grandchildren. There was one of Mrs. Donnelly posing with a man on her wedding day.

He opened the bathroom door and saw her lying on her side. She was wearing a lilac dressing gown, but its belt was splayed across the tiles like an umbilical cord, and when he saw her sagging breasts peeping between the fabric he quickly turned away.

'I'm sorry,' he said. 'I didn't realise...'

'Don't be daft. I'd rather it be you than the milkman.'

He put a hand under each armpit and heaved her to her feet.

'I slipped when I was doing my teeth. Christ alive, Doug – thank God you came to check.'

He took her to the living room and sat her on the couch. Before he could ask her if she needed anything, she told him there were some leftover faggots waiting for him in the fridge.

By the time the doctor had been round to check on Mrs. Donnelly it was nearly 1am.

'Thank you so much for tonight, Doug – you've been an absolute angel you have.'

He tapped her on the shoulder as if testing a fence for electricity. 'No worries,' he said. 'I'm happy to help.'

But that night he couldn't sleep. He was stuck between dreams and the contours of his bedroom. The door was a forest opening; the table of native weapons was a desk stacked with porno mags and empty cans of deodorant. He too felt empty. Not in a bad way, just weightless and detached. He felt like Colonel Kurtz, protected from the world by the valleys of south Wales.

At 6am he got up and went to the supermarket. He returned with two carriers bags stuffed with frozen chicken and Tesco value tins, and a cardboard box containing something called a CrockPot – the boys at The Foal had been talking about it months, and he supposed it could come in handy at some point, anyway.

He threw the whole lot in – chicken, kidney beans, onion, vegetable stock – and spent the next few hours watching *Mutiny on the Bounty* and keeping his fingers crossed.

Finally, it was lunchtime. He checked. He thought it tasted ok.

He descended the stairs to Mrs. Donnelly's flat and knocked on her door. When she saw him, her eyes lit up like the power button on the pressure cooker.

'Oh Doug, thank you so much. Looks bloody beautiful, it does.'

He handed her a plastic container containing a portion of casserole, on top a get well card for which he couldn't find the envelope.

'Come in – we can eat together.'

He stepped inside her flat and she directed him to the kitchen. It didn't take much effort to pretend that he hadn't already eaten his share.

*

'So tomorrow's your first day back at The Foal,' she says. Mrs. Donnelly is already onto her second caramel latte, but Dougie's still fishing the seeds and oats from his first.

For a moment he's silent. 'Actually… tomorrow there's a new film on in the cinema I'd quite like to see. I was wondering if you'd like to go?'

'Tomorrow?' she replies. 'I thought you'd be busy – don't you want to enjoy your first proper pint in a month?'

'Well, I've been thinking about it, and I've decided that it won't be that much fun down there if I'm constantly walking on egg-shells. I'd rather be doing something else, to be honest…'

He studies her face; the way it seems to reveal its secrets over the course of a conversation. Her eyes seem greener in the day than at night.

'Yeah,' she says. 'Sounds good to me, Doug.'

They set a time and he downs the rest of his coffee. When they step out onto the high street and make their way back to their apartment building, he wonders if his own face reveals secrets that even he has yet to discover.

Daniel Williams

Riding an Elephant

'I wish I'd ridden an elephant,' confessed Mo as she massaged her knee. 'Sometimes, I sit here and imagine I'm sat atop one. It's just me, the elephant and the sunset.' Mo stared into nothing and imagined the setting sun, the mountains, and the closing of the day. She thought about the elephant, strolling along the almost hidden dirt path whilst waving its wrinkled trunk. It would be beautiful to do something so peaceful. Mo tilted her head back and with a softened voice whispered, 'Me and my elegant elephant.'

Exhaling slowly in comfort, Mo peeled herself off her chair and reached for her cane. Her grandson Patrick, sitting on her bed, offered his help as his grandmother trudged over to the window. 'I can do it Patrick,' cracked Mo, leaning on the windowsill gasping for breath. 'I'm okay, love.'

Mo always looked forward to Patrick's weekly visit; Sunday afternoon, just after two. He's busy, but he makes time for his grandmother. This week Patrick wanted to surprise his gran and had called in to see her on the Wednesday. He knew she got lonely sometimes, spending most of her time in her room, flicking through old photo albums and watching the passers-by going about their day.

'Never made the most of it see. If only I was twenty again like you,' Mo tells Patrick as she spies out on the courtyard, spotting some of her fellow residents lounging by the willow tree and giving them a wave. 'Too late now of course, I could've done so many things, I threw away all those chances.' Mo looked at Patrick and saw his face smiling back at her. She waved her finger at him and ordered him to 'Make the most of it, love.'

'Okay, Gran.' Patrick smiled a half smile which stretched up towards his left cheek and he headed for the kettle. 'Cuppa?' Mo muttered a yes, plumped up her cushion and sat back down in the armchair.

'You know this was your grandfather's armchair, don't you? I'm leaving this to you when I go, I know you'd like that.'

'Come on, Gran, don't say things like that.' Patrick dropped the spoon onto the worktop. 'You're not going anywhere.'

'Ah that's just it see, I know exactly when I will die, I've known since the fifties.' Mo, in complete confidence, nodded as she told her grandson.

'What do you mean you've known since the fifties? You've never told me about this.'

'I haven't wanted to worry you, Paddy. But it's my birthday next week and it's time I told you.' Patrick, through a mouthful of tea-soaked digestive, urged his gran to carry on. 'I was seventeen, and all the boys wanted me—'

'Gran,' interrupted Patrick, dropping his voice low.

'Okay, okay, forget that bit then. It's true though,' Mo smirked, winking at Patrick. 'It was a hot summer's night and I was going out with the girls. This was the fifties, the good old days. My father had treated me to a whole new outfit, a new tea dress, navy, with a floral pattern, and a pair of kitten heels. Fashionable see.' She reached into the drawer beside her and pulled out a photo album. Its corners were scuffed and a few photographs were missing, but it was held together by a glossy red ribbon. Mo carefully slid a photograph out of its place, flattened its dog-eared edges and pointed. 'There I am that very night, Paddy. See there, that's me on the end.' After taking a few minutes looking at the photograph and naming the other people in it, telling Patrick each and every one of their fates, she continued.

'The night was fantastic; we went down to the pier and spent all of our pocket money in the penny arcade and on milkshakes.' Mo sipped her tea and stared into the swirling greasy layer floating at the top. 'Time catches you up before you know it, Paddy. Can you believe that's me there,' pointing at the photo again, 'bonkers isn't it love?'

Patrick scratched his head and asked, 'What's all this about knowing when you'll, you know,' Patrick coughed, 'die.'

'Well, just as we were about to leave the pier that night, one of the girls suggested that we go and see a psychic. They always had them on the pier, and we were enjoying ourselves, so we went along. I'd never been to a psychic before, didn't believe in all that stuff, but it wasn't going to hurt.' Mo finished the last drops of her tea and struggled over to the window again, this time wiping a smudge off the pane with her handkerchief.

'Helen was told that she would fall in love within the month, Margaret that she'd have a baby soon, and Sandra was told that she was adopted – no it wasn't Sandra, it was Sarah.' Mo, still by the window turned to Patrick to make sure he was still listening. 'When the three of them came out and told me that, I laughed, well it was quite funny, and we didn't believe that anyone could possibly know all of that.' Mo let out a chuckle before stopping to continue. 'But, strangely enough, the psychic was right. Helen found love, Margaret fell pregnant that summer and Sarah's parents confirmed that she was adopted.'

'Really?' Patrick sat there open mouthed. 'You're pulling my leg.'

'No, no, God's honest truth.'

'It can't be, you've been taken for a fool.'

'Don't you believe me, love?' Mo raised her voice. 'I wouldn't lie to you Patrick, here's the proof.'

'Okay Gran, sorry. So, what did the psychic say to you?'

Mo straightened up her woollen cardigan and replied, 'She told me I would live until I was –' there was a pause, and after taking a deep breath and smacking her lips Mo continued, '–eighty-one, and that on my eighty-first birthday, I would leave this world for the next.'

'But you turn eighty-one next week.' Patrick put his tea on the bedside table in a panic.

'Yes, and I've been thinking a lot about that these past few months. I've been thinking back at all the good times, and all the bad, everything makes you who you are, Paddy. I feel like I'm ready now, it feels like time.' Mo glanced at the photo of her and her late husband on their wedding day which was hanging above the television and apologised to Patrick. Such morbid talk. 'I've had a good life, Patrick, and I'm so grateful for it all, but I know I could have done so much more.'

Patrick shook his head, 'It's okay Gran, I don't believe in that old psychic nonsense, you're perfectly fit and healthy. You'll be here much longer than you think. Besides, I thought I'd take you out next week, maybe for a meal, you know, to celebrate.' Mo tightened her lips and thanked Patrick.

'Oh, where's the time gone, you better get going, you coming down Sunday like normal, love?'

'Yes of course, two o'clock on Sunday.' Patrick stood up, kissed his gran on her cheek and collected his things, reassuring himself and his gran that she wasn't going anywhere.

The next day, Patrick picked up a box of hazelnut toffees and a bunch of daisies, his gran's favourites, and headed to see her. Their conversation the day before had made him want to see her sooner than the Sunday. Patrick knocked, but there was no answer. As he entered he realised that the room was empty. His gran's immaculately made bed stood proudly in the centre of the room with sunlight beaming through the window onto the plaid quilt. 'Gran?' he whispered, with only the sound of the dripping tap answering him. Nothing. Patrick spotted a letter leaning against the pillow on the bed, his stomach landed on the floor and he rushed over to the bed flinging the flowers and toffees onto the armchair.

The letter was addressed to Patrick, a perfectly presented envelope, with a wax seal, something Patrick had only ever seen before in films. He ripped the fold open and broke the wax seal in one swift slide. With his eyes getting teary, Patrick took a breath in anticipation, and read the letter.

My dear Patrick,

Thank you for coming to visit me so often, I am extremely grateful.

I was thinking about the conversation we had last time I saw you, and how I was telling you to take every chance you get. Well, I haven't exactly lived by that rule, so I thought, who am I to tell you?

My friends really did have all those things happen to them, and even though I've believed all this time that I will die on my eighty-first birthday I have never really lived life to the full.

But I'm not going without fulfilling my dream.

Look after your grandfather's armchair and look after yourself.

I'll see you again,

Gran

P.S. I'm riding an elephant now.

Acknowledgements

Through the encouragement of Jo Furber, Literature Officer at the Dylan Thomas Centre, Alan Kellermann, Amanda O'Neill, Alan and Jean Perry, the Terry Hetherington Young Writers Award was established in the namesake of my late partner, Terry Hetherington, who died in 2007. It is thanks to Neath Port Talbot Community Voluntary Service that we are registered as a voluntary trust.

Thank you to the trustees for their ongoing support; Phil Knight (Chairman), Amanda O'Neill (Secretary), Huw Pudner (Promotions Officer), Liza Osborne, Kirsty Parsons, Rose Widlake, Glyn Edwards and Jonathan Edwards.

Malcolm Lloyd provides the most comprehensive website. It details all past prize winners, details about the award, videos of past awards evenings, videos of Poems and Pints, events and latest news. *Cheval* books are for sale, as well as the books published in the namesake of past prize-winners. Malcolm also administers entries to the award and ensures the entries remain anonymous to the judges. His dedication is enormous.

The main source of fundraising is through the dedication of contributors to *Cheval*: Neath Poems and Pints, held every month at the Cambrian Arms in Melyn. We are especially grateful to the proprietors Dewi, Gavin and Colin. Neath Town Council provide a grant in aid towards activities for

Poems and Pints.

Other sources of funding are especially appreciated from past prize winner Chris Hyatt, Jen and Mike Wilson, Margot Morgan, Gwenda Lloyd, Byron Beynon, Ioan Richard, Patrick Dobbs and Margaret Webley. Tokens for the awards evening raffle come from Tesco store Neath Abbey, and Clarks Shoes. Books are donated by Richard Lewis Davies of Parthian Books and Sally Roberts Jones of Alun Books.

Year after year, friends of the late Terry Hetherington attend the awards evening and Poems and Pints, purchasing books and buying raffle tickets. They are Dave and Gwyneth Hughes, Amber Hiscott, members of the Owain Glyndwr Society, Liz Hobbs, Steve Croke, Marian Frances, Dewi Bowen, Robert King, Mike Jenkins, David Williams, Gabriella and Humberto, Linda Kinsey, Mike Burrows and Patrick Dobbs.

The dedication and skills of the editors of *Cheval 12* are very much appreciated, past prize winners of the Terry Hetherington Young Writers Award; Rose Widlake and Glyn Edwards. Also, the skills of the publisher Parthian Books, and help from Molly Holborn and Eddie Matthews.

Thank you to musicians Huw Pudner, Bob Thomas and Brendan Barker.

We are grateful to volunteers: for filming and photography, Michael O'Neill; Nathan and Katie for selling raffle tickets; providing prizes, Liza Osborne and Buddug Hughes; for helping to organise the evening, Kym Barker, Amanda and Kirsty and Phil Knight.

Thanks to the dedication and staff at the Dylan Thomas Centre.

We are delighted with the social network of young writers who attend the awards evenings, provide help and promotion of other writers at the awards evening and on facebook; Natalie Holborn, Georgia Carys Williams, Sion Tomos Owen, Tyler Keevil, Anna Lewis, Rhian Elizabeth, Mari Ellis Dunning, Joao Morais, Lowri Llewelyn, Michael Oliver Seminov, and Thomas Tyrrell.

Aida Birch

Author Biographies

Eleanor Howe Eleanor is originally from Derbyshire. She is currently living in north Wales in a beautiful old barge. She writes about nature and landscape. Eleanor's non-fiction and critical work has been published online. *Cheval 12* has brought her the opportunity for her creative work to be published.

Nathan Munday Nathan is currently living in a remote valley in Snowdonia. He completed his doctorate in literature last September. His travel book, *Seven Days: A Pyrenean Adventure*, published by Parthian in 2017, was a runner up in New Welsh Writing Awards 2016. Nathan has been published in previous *Cheval* anthologies, as well as *New Welsh Review*.

Cynan Llwyd Cynan lives in Cardiff. He is published in *Cheval 10*, also in the Welsh language in a collection *Byd Crwm*, published by Y Lolfa. He has a novel for children currently being published, also by Y Lolfa. Cynan works for Christian Aid as a regional Coordinator. His writing is inspired by people he meets here in Wales, and all over the world. He strives to fight for an end to poverty.

Morgan Owen Morgan is a bilingual poet and essayist. He usually writes in the Welsh language. Morgan is inspired by the mutability and diversity of spaces and the ways in which spaces interact. He finds Wales offers a startling interaction of spaces. He has a Masters degree in Welsh and Celtic studies. His work regularly appears in; *Barddas, O'r Pedwar Gwynt* and *Y Stamp*. In January 2019 Morgan was Radio Cymru'r Poet of the month (Bardd y Mis). His own collection should be available soon.

Katya Johnson Katya gained her doctorate in Creative Writing at Aberystwyth University in 2018. In the same year Katya was awarded first prize for the Terry Hetherington Young Writers Award. Her writing explores ways in which human identity is shaped by the environment. Her work has been published in *Cheval 11*. She was awarded second prize winner in 2017 and published in *Cheval 10*. Katya has also been published in *New Welsh Review, Poetry Wales* and *New Writing*.

Gareth Smith Gareth is currently completing a Ph.D in English Literature. His work has been published in several previous *Cheval* anthologies. He had a short play performed for the Sherman Cymru's 40th Anniversary celebrations, and was shortlisted for a BBC writing competition

Samuel Hulett Samuel is originally from the Rhymney Valley. He studied Biology at Swansea University, and he is currently studying for an MA in Creative Writing with the Open University. He currently lives in Cardiff; he works for a children's rights charity, but loves getting out of Cardiff and into the mountains.

Kathy Chamberlain Kathy is originally from Plymouth. Last year she gained her doctorate at Swansea University. Kathy teaches undergraduates in Creative Writing, and English Literature. Her role at the University challenges her to keep abreast of exciting new writing. Kathy is published in several of the previous *Cheval* anthologies.

Catrin Lawrence Catrin is an undergraduate student at Swansea University. She is studying Creative Writing and English Literature. Catrin wrote her first story when she was just five years old. The story was about a lost starfish. Her enthusiasm for writing continued, and she is delighted to see her name in print in *Cheval 12*.

Cara Cullen Cara studied history at the University of Oxford. She is a writer, musician and artist. Her studies have included Welsh History, violin performance at Trinity Laban, and she sings and performs with 5-string banjo. Cara works at St. Fagans National Museum. Her poem 'Cil-stone', (Cil is a Welsh word meaning corner) is about one of the houses in St Fagans called 'Cilwent'. It was moved to the museum after the flooding of the Elan valley.

Ashleigh Davies Ashleigh lives in Monmouthsire, and is a graduate of Cardiff Metropolitan University. His writing has appeared in *Poetry Wales*, The *New Welsh Reader* and *Haverthorn*, among other publications. Several of Ashleigh's poems are published in *Cheval 11*. Follow him on twitter@asleighrdavies

Megan Thomas Megan completed a BA in English, Media and Journalism at the University of Cape Town, having grown up in Johannesburg, South Africa. Megan achieved an MA in Creative Writing from Cardiff University. She has a passion for slightly twisted short stories. Her ambition is to work in publishing, whilst continuing to write fiction.

Josh Weeks Josh is from Caldicot. He is currently studying for a Ph.D in Latin American literature at the University of Amsterdam. He has been published in *Ellipsis Zine*, *Five 2 One* Magazine, and *Cheval 11*. He is also working as an English teacher. One of his short stories will be included in an anthology to be released under the Amsterdam indle print, Otherwhere.

Aaron Farrell Aaron is from Bangor where he is studying Creative and Professional Writing at Bangor University. He is a Film Critic for Ready, Steady, Cut and Nation Cymru, Young Critic for the Arts Council of Wales. He is currently writing a novel representing working-class travellers through semi-autobiographical fiction.

Eve Moriarty Eve is originally from Lancashire. She is a researcher and Creative Writing PhD candidate at Swansea University. Eve was awarded a Literature Wales bursary to work on her collection *Radium Girls*, and won second prize in the 2015 Robin Reeves award. Eve has been published in several *Cheval* anthologies.

Saoirse O'Connor Saoirse's childhood was spent in Buckinghamshire, and she is currently living in Cardiff where she is at university. Saoirse commences a Master's Degree in Creative Writing in September. Since commencing her degree she attends the English Literature Society open mics. She mostly writes about her own experiences in life.

James Lloyd James is a Gwynedd based writer who studied Creative Writing and Film Studies at Bangor University. His writing never strays far from landscape, the foundation for our understanding of home. He is published in *Cheval 11*, *The*

Cardiff Review and *Wales Arts Review*. He tweets @JamesLloydWrite

Jaffrin Khan Jaffrin lives in Cardiff. He is studying for a degree in English, and he commenced creative writing through reflecting identity. He transforms pieces of prose writing into poetry. Jaffrin attends Spoken Word performances.

Jack Rendell Jack is a graduate of Aberystwyth University, and has achieved a Masters Degree in Creative Writing. He writes poetry and fantasy fiction. He is published in several previous *Cheval* anthologies, and is currently writing a novel.

Emily Cotterill Emily is originally from Alfreton, Derbyshire, and moved to Cardiff in 2010 to study at the university. She graduated in 2013 and has continued to write. She writes about a sense of meaning and place. Emily's debut pamphlet; *The Day of the Flying Ants* will be published in May 2019. Her work is also published in *Cheval 11*.

Kelly Bishop Kelly is a Creative Writing and Media graduate from Cardiff Metropolitan University. She is currently undertaking a Masters Degree in Specialist Journalism. Writing poetry helps Kelly to overcome anxiety and appreciate the Arts.

Taylor Edmonds Taylor is a writer and poet from Barry. She is currently studying for a Masters Degree in Creative Writing at Cardiff University. Her work has been published in *Wales Arts Review, Butcher's Dog* magazine, as well as *The Cardiff Review, Lucent Dreaming* magazine, and more widely. Taylor also participates in Spoken Word performance.

Eluned Gramich Eluned is a past prize winner of the Terry Hetherington Young Writers Award, and she is a writer and translator. Her memoir of Hokkaido, *Woman Who Brings the Rain* won the New Welsh Writing Award 2015 and was shortlisted for Wales Book of the Year. Eluned has lived in Japan and Germany and is currently studying Creative Writing for a PhD at Aberystwyth University

Emily Green Emily is a writer and English lecturer who gained a Masters Degree at Cardiff University. She has had short stories and flash fiction published in anthologies, as well as *Cheval 10*. She was highly commended for the Robin Reeves Prize for young writers in 2015. She is currently writing an auto ethnographic article for publication in an academic textbook about the relationship between social class and academia.

Theo Elwyn Hung Theo is a freelance writer and full-time Stage Manager, hailing from Hong Kong, and is currently working in Wales. He is published in *Buzz* magazine and *Wales Arts Review*. Theo finds writing is liberating and aims to continue writing for many days to come.

Jonathan Macho Jonathan lives in Cardiff. He has an English Literature degree, and is published in three of the *To Hull and Back* short story anthologies, in three issues of the *404 INK* literary magazine, as well as in the *Cheval 10* anthology. He is inspired by the 'uncanny'. He has contributed to plays and comics, and intends to continue writing for as long as he can.

Rhea Seren Phillips Rhea is studying for a PhD at Swansea University and is researching Welsh poetic traditions in the English language. She is widely published in *Welsh Innovative*

Poetry, Poetry Wales, Envoi, The Lonely Crowd, Gogoneddus Ych-a-Fi ; an exhibition of work by contemporary Surrealists (2018) *Molly Bloom* (2018), as well as *Cheval 10* and *11*. She contributes regularly to 'Parallel Cymru', a bilingual project website; https://parallel.cymru/poets/. Follow Rhea on Twitter @rhea_seren

Laura Mae Satterthwaite Laura is the youngest contributor for 2019 Young Writers Award. She is currently completing her 'A' levels, and she has a confirmed place at Cardiff University to study English Literature and History. Laura is from Llandudno Junction in north Wales. She began writing as a form of emotional release, and writing has become a huge part of her life.

Samuel A. Verdin Samuel is a writer currently studying Creative Writing at Bangor University. He is an aspiring author and has several works of short fiction published in short fiction magazines such as *Bare Fiction* and *Dead Bird Review*. He is currently building a new, innovative review platform. Samuel particularly enjoys the art of storytelling. He has staged at Edinburgh's Fringe Festival.

Daniel Williams Daniel is from Port Talbot and works as an English teacher at a comprehensive school in Cowbridge. He particularly enjoys writing creatively, but sadly his occupation as a teacher leaves very little time for his own writing. However, his passion for writing is helping to inspire young talent by setting up a Creative Writing Club at the school where he is teaching. Daniel has been published in *Cheval 10*.

Laura James-Brownsell Laura is a MArts Creative Writing student. She is studying with the University of Wales, Trinity Saint David, at Lampeter. She is currently working on producing her second novel. Laura is particularly concerned about climate change and tries to reflect this in her fiction.

Millie Meader Millie lives near Hengoed, mid Glamorgan and is an avid reader of Gothic and Romantic works. She has a very special interest in local history and the regeneration projects involved. Millie's fiction reflects on her interests as a writer.

Caragh Medlicott Caragh lives in Cardiff. She is a writer with a First Class degree in English Literature and has a Masters degree in Creative Writing. Her work is regularly published in *Wales Arts Review*.